MW01603150

# COUNTDOWN TO ARMAGEDDON

**Darrell Maloney**

Copyright 2014 by Darrell Maloney

Please check out Darrell Maloney's best selling book,

**_The Secession of Texas_**

As well as his other fine works, available at
Amazon.com and at Barnes and Noble Booksellers.

This book is dedicated to three very special ladies in my life: Eleanor Barrick, Dawn Brand Hawkins and Qe Terry. Without their encouragement and support, I would not have started writing again. These stories would be trapped in my head forever. Thank you, my friends…

# -1-

Scott Harter wasn't special by anybody's standards. He wasn't a handsome guy at all. He wasn't dumb, but he'd never win a Nobel Prize either. He had no hidden talents, although he fancied himself a fairly good karaoke singer.

His friends didn't necessarily share that opinion, but what did they know?

No, if those friends were tasked to choose one word to describe Scott Harter, that word might well be "average."

If Scott excelled at one thing, it was that he was a very good businessman. And he was also a lot luckier than most.

And it was that combination – his penchant for making a buck, and being lucky, that led him here on this day to the Guerra Public Library on the west side of San Antonio.

To research what he believed was the pending collapse of mankind.

Twenty three years earlier, in 1990, Scott had done two things that would change his life forever. Even back then, he was just an average Joe. He'd had plans to become a doctor, but his average grades weren't cutting it. So he dropped out of college halfway through his junior year.

He'd have loved to have married a beauty queen, but his average looks certainly did nothing to attract any. Neither did his average amount of charm. So instead he started dating Linda Amparano, who was a sweet girl but somewhat average herself. They seemed to make a perfect, if slightly vanilla, couple.

The second thing Scott had done that year was buy a dilapidated self-storage unit on the north side of San Antonio. It was one of those places where people rent lockers to store their things when their garages have run out of space. Or their kids go off to college. Or when they just accumulate so many things that they've run out of room to put them all.

Pat, the guy who'd sold the property to Scott, was a friendly enough sort, but not a businessman at all. He didn't understand some of the basic principles of running such an operation.

Not that Scott was an expert. At least back then he wasn't.

But even back then, Scott knew the value of curb appeal, and that a fresh paint job and a few repairs could attract a few more customers. And a few more customers would help supply money for advertising, and special offers, and long-term lease discounts. No brainers, actually.

So by the end of that year, two things had happened. Scott had turned around the business and turned it into a money-making operation. And he had married Linda.

The pair had said their vows on December 17th of that year. It was bitterly cold that day. The coldest December 17th on record for that part of Texas.

If the cold was an omen, though, neither of them saw it. If either of them had, and had gotten cold feet, their lives would be so much different today.

But they just laughed it off, as young couples in love are wont to do. And they went ahead with their nuptials and started their lives together and never looked back at that cold day in December when they ran headlong into a marriage that shouldn't have happened.

The marriage lasted nine years. It produced two great sons, so there was that. And Scott and Linda remained friends. That was something else. So there was a good legacy, of sorts, left behind by their mistake that cold December day.

Scott adored his boys. There was Jordan, his oldest, who was intelligent and talented and a bit of a goofball. And there was Zachary, who Scott was convinced would someday become a scientist or a highly successful engineer. Zach was always taking things apart and making other things with them. His curious mind never stopped working, and he loved exploring new things and new ideas. Zach was sweeter than a bucket of molasses. He was everybody's best friend.

Yes, Scott was lucky as a father. No problems with his boys at all.

He was also lucky in that he lived in Texas at the time of the divorce. Texas wasn't an alimony state. So he wasn't saddled with monster alimony payments like his brother in Atlanta was. His brother Mike was divorced the same year as Scott, and was ordered by the court to pay forty percent of his before-tax income to a wife who had cheated on him multiple times.

No, Scott had no such problem. He helped Linda financially occasionally when she fell behind. It was the right thing to do. And he doted on his boys and bought them nice things.

But since he didn't have to pay alimony, he was able to take that money instead and use it to build his business.

After the first storage facility was turning a healthy profit, he was able to buy a second. Then a third. And with each one he followed the same business model. He'd do some cosmetic improvements to attract a few more customers. Then he'd turn that additional income into air time on the local radio station, or ads in the local paper. Getting the word out drew more customers, which in turn would supply more money for special deals and discounts. Which would provide more money for another new facility.

It was a business model that had served him well.

And now, twenty three years later, Scott Harter owned a chain of thirty one storage facilities spread throughout San Antonio and nearby Houston.

So even though he wasn't as handsome as a movie star, and would never be a candidate to join Mensa, he was doing all right. And that was good enough for him.

Linda had remarried within a year. The marriage only lasted two years and was full of problems. She waited a bit longer to marry her third husband, and the third time seemed to be the charm for her. The third husband, Tony, was a good man, who treated Linda and the boys well. At least it appeared that way to Tony. He didn't know that since their divorce, Linda had gotten very good at putting on airs and keeping secrets. Keeping the ugly truth from Scott made it easier for Scott and Tony to be casual friends. Scott eventually found out that Tony was a con man and a user, who'd taken Linda for pretty much everything she had.

It was Scott who helped her get back on her feet. She banished Tony from her life, and swore off marriage forever.

From that point on, Linda chose a life less complicated. A life with an endless stream of boyfriends who didn't provide a sense of stability. But they were a lot easier to get rid of when they didn't work out.

Their boys had been brought up in a stable environment, which meant they were well behaved and relatively problem free. Neither of them ever got into drugs, or ran away from home. Neither of them had gone to jail, or left a string of broken hearts. Both of them were good kids, who had bright futures ahead of them. Or so they thought. Actually, there were problems ahead, which none of them knew about, but which their father would soon discover.

Yes, all in all, Scott was a lucky man, despite his being just an average guy. And he was living a pretty comfortable life.

That was about to change.

## -2-

"How about the ten by ten, number 32?" Scott asked his office manager Stacy. "Are they six months delinquent yet?"

Stacy answered "No, not quite yet. They will be on Wednesday. I've been trying to get hold of the guy, but his home phone's been disconnected, and he never provided us a cell phone number."

"Did you try his work number?"

"Yes, and all they'll tell me is that he no longer works there."

Another thing Scott had in common with the average Joes of the world was his penchant for doing things a little bit shady sometimes. As a businessman, he should hate it when one of his clients failed to make their rental payments for six months and thereby defaulted on their contracts. Scott was happy, though. Each time it happened, he saw it as an opportunity.

The law was very specific. If anyone got six months or more behind, and could not be contacted to make arrangements to pick up their things and pay their back rent, then their things became the property of the storage company.

The typical disposition, of course, would be to sell the contents of such lockers at auction, just like all the shows on the cable channels.

And Scott did that. In most cases, that is. But the shady side of his character, the side that few people saw, was the side that would compel him to come late at night, unbeknownst to his employees or anyone else, to check out each such locker to see what was in it.

Scott had a habit of waiting until Stacy or one of his other managers would go home, then going to each newly defaulted locker. He'd cut the padlock and crack the locker open, and dig through everything to see what he could find that would be of any value to him.

Then he'd make a decision to either keep the contents of the locker himself, or to put another lock on it and sell it at auction for what typically may only be a few hundred dollars.

Over the years he'd amassed a considerable amount of treasures through this particular bad habit. He hadn't bought a watch in twenty years, having found enough Rolexes and Cartiers to keep him supplied. The same was true of his Oakley sunglasses and Callaway golf clubs.

And a side business. He had a very successful antique and collectibles store in the heart of San Antonio, just blocks from the Alamo. Completely stocked by the old furniture items, autographed baseballs and fine china he'd recovered from defaulted lockers.

In his own mind, he was doing nothing wrong. After all, it wasn't like he was taking all the good stuff out of the lockers and then auctioning off the leftover junk to an unwitting bidder. No, indeed, if he found things of value, he just declined to offer that particular locker in the auction. He himself kept it, purged it of its valuables, and then carted the rest of the stuff to the landfill.

The bidders at his auctions, of course, didn't know anything about Scott's habit. So they'd come to the auctions, hoping to hit it big, to buy a locker that had a forgotten Picasso inside, or a hidden stash of hundred dollar bills. And when it never happened, they just assumed it wasn't their lucky day. It never occurred to them that Scott had already claimed the good lockers, and that their dream payday had no chance of happening.

Scott made a note to himself to come back on Thursday night after Stacy had gone home and check out locker 32.

He knew it had belonged to a professor at nearly St. Mary's University. Professors sometimes had valuable artifacts or rare books that they showed their students at some point during a course. Then they typically got put away for the next group of young minds. Scott was hoping to find such items in the old professor's locker.

On Thursday, just before 11 p.m., Scott cracked open number 32 and flipped on the light. The mess and disarray he saw didn't surprise him. College professors could be quite disorganized, and even a little eccentric. So the fact that everything wasn't all neatly boxed and organized was certainly no shock. What was curious, though, was the nature of the contents.

There were stacks and stacks of reference books and novels, all having to do with the Mayan culture. Posters of the Mayan calendar. Boxes of printed paper that appeared to be research material. Three telescopes of various sizes. A huge chart of the universe, rolled up and leaning against the wall.

Scott was a bit upset with himself for wasting his time. There was nothing in this locker of any real value. He'd be lucky to get fifty bucks for it at the next auction.

Then something caught his eye.

It rested atop a stack of boxes, but looked a bit out of place. It was a hardcover book, an ugly green in color. But it had no title on either its face or spine. No words at all to indicate what might be inside.

He opened it up and found that it was a ledger, of the type used by accountants and bookkeepers to keep track of numbers. The pages were each divided into columns, meant to keep track of funds, or debits or credits or whatever figures people keep track of.

But this ledger contained no numbers.

Rather, it appeared to be a diary.

Scott started to read.


*"I've come to the conclusion that Professor Maribel was right. The Mayans somehow figured out how to predict solar flare activity. I mean, is it so far fetched to believe that such a thing is possible, with all the other things this mysterious society was able to accomplish?*

*"People of science go on and on about the Egyptians and their achievements. People of history point to the Romans and the Greeks and talk of their contributions to the modern world.*

*"In my opinion, the Greeks, Romans and Egyptians had nothing on the Mayans.*

*"While the world was freaking out about the whole Mayan calendar thing, they missed the whole point. The*

*Mayans never said that the world was going to end on Dec 21st, 2012. They merely marked that date as the start of a new period in human existence. The final period of progress, they called it.*

*"So the world isn't going to end, in the big ball of flames that people believe.*

*"Rather, mankind will continue to survive, but in a vastly different world. A world without machines or technology."*

Scott walked into the cavernous Guerra Library not quite knowing where to start.

The professor had hinted at a monumental disaster about to overcome mankind. But he only left a few vague clues. Sunspot activities... solar storms... large scale destruction of anything electronic.

Professor Mason had also left a few clues that, if used properly, could minimize the effects of the catastrophe. Something called a Foley cage... stockpiling of essentials... learning not to rely on mechanical things or processes.

Scott was fascinated, while at the same time a little bit unnerved. Whoever this professor was, he must be pretty smart, or he wouldn't be a professor, right?

Scott's world was sometimes broken down into simple components. But he was a successful businessman, after all. And he got where he was by trusting his instincts and his gut.

And his gut told him that Professor Mason went through a lot of time and trouble writing about this coming catastrophe. And that Scott had better pay damn close attention if he wanted to have a leg up on everyone else when the catastrophe came about.

So every day for the better part of three weeks Scott found the articles and theses quoted in Professor Mason's notes. And he made notes of his own.

And in the end, he believed what the old Professor had believed. That the Mayans weren't saying the end of the world was going to happen on December 21, 2012. They were saying that's when the earth entered the cycle of solar activity that would make it most vulnerable to being bombarded with a huge storm of electronic magnetic pulses, which would short out anything electric or electronic. And would essentially send earth back to the stone age.

The Mayans, it turned out, were a lot more advanced than most people gave them credit for. Scientists had known for a hundred years that the Mayans had identified all the planets and constellations in the sky, even though they had no telescopes. They learned how to predict earthquakes although they had none of the fancy equipment that scientists had today. Scientists who despite that fancy equipment still can't predict earthquakes.

The Mayans could also predict tidal waves, simply by calculating the movements of the planets and their relationship to the tidal pull of the moon at any given time. Modern day scientists knew the Mayans had the capability of doing that, they just didn't know how.

So it wasn't a stretch, then, when the Mayans said certain things were going to happen on the surface of the sun sometime in the next few years, not to scoff at their predictions. It made good sense to believe it, and to take some precautions. Not precautions to stop the disaster, for it was unstoppable.

No, Scott would start taking precautions to mitigate the damage done to him and his family when the disaster happened. He'd make sure they were prepared to survive what few others could.

He walked out of the library that last day with a mission. It was a mission he was afraid to tell anyone about, because he knew they'd think him crazy. And perhaps he was. After all, he didn't know anything at all about this mysterious Professor Mason... who he was, where he came from, or whether he was alive or dead. But by reading the professor's notes and doing his own research, he was now a believer.

A believer that sometime in the next few years, a huge solar storm would erupt on the surface of the sun. It would create massive sunspots not seen since the introduction of electricity in the late 1800s. And the solar activity would send electromagnetic pulses, or EMPs, to bombard the earth and to short out virtually anything electric.

Unless those things were protected.

Something else Scott learned while in the library was that there are certain ways to protect electrical items from EMPs. It wouldn't be easy. But he was determined. And when the solar storm happened, and the world went black, Scott and his family would be spared the misery the rest of the world would be enduring. While the rest of the world was learning to live in the stone age, Scott and his family would still be living in relative comfort.

He had a lot of work to do, and not much time to do it. Actually, that part was not necessarily true. According to the Mayans, the window was now open. But they left no clues to show how big that window was. The storms could arrive twelve years from now. Or, they could arrive tomorrow.

Scott, unable to predict exactly when the chaos would occur, knew he had no time to waste.

# -3-

"I'm calling about a tract of land you posted up in the hill country, south of Junction," Scott told the realtor over the phone. "Is it still available?"

He could almost hear the hunger in Joyce Allen's voice as she jumped at the chance to discuss the old Ryan place. It had been on the market for three years, since old man Ryan died, and had come down in price three times, without so much as a nibble.

"Yes, sir. Yes, sir indeed. It is a bit rugged and isolated, but perfect for someone looking to escape the big city. Can I get your name?"

"Scott Harter. I live in San Antonio, in the King's Estates."

Joyce scribbled his name on a scratch pad with a large question mark and slid the pad over to an associate at the next desk. The associate didn't even have to ask what it meant. She and Joyce had been realtors in the same land office for many years. They could read each other's minds. So while Joyce chatted up Mr. Harter, the associate would do a quick search on him to determine his financial standing and credit rating. It would tell Joyce whether she was wasting her time speaking to a man who had neither the means nor the desire to purchase a million dollar piece of rural land seventy miles north of San Antonio.

If the associate came back after five minutes and handed the note back to Joyce with a big "X" across it, Joyce would cut the conversation short and let the old Ryan place languish in real estate purgatory for a few more years.

But on the other hand, if the note were modified by the associate to include a large happy face, Joyce would suddenly become Mr. Harter's new best friend. Would go on and on about the merits of the Ryan place. How it was heaven on earth. Isolated, yes. But at $1.2 million, a steal by anybody's standards.

It only took four minutes this time. The associate was getting faster. Joyce made a mental note to take her to lunch when the note slid back across the desk to her.

Not only a happy face, but a happy face followed by three very large exclamation marks.

"I'll tell you what, Mr. Harter. This piece of land cannot be adequately described over the phone. It has to be seen to be appreciated. Would you like to make an appointment to see the property in person, perhaps bring your wife and family and make a morning of it?"

Joyce smiled and gave the associate a high five.

Scott answered, "Well, there is no wife. I've been divorced for several years. And my boys will be in school. But I can meet you up there at say, nine a.m. tomorrow if that's convenient."

"Oh, yes of course, Mr. Harter. Nine would be perfect. Do you know how to get there?"

"Yes. The directions on your web site are quite specific, and I've already looked at the Google Earth satellite photos of it. I believe it may be just the type of property I'm looking for."

"Perfect. Thank you for your call, then, Mr. Harter. I look forward to seeing you at nine a.m. tomorrow."

Joyce hung up the phone and shouted "Yes!" to no one in particular. Then she stood up and hugged the associate, and sat back down to calculate twenty two percent of $1.2 million. The Ryan family had promised a twenty two percent commission to whichever lucky realtor was able to dump the old man's place. It had become a family albatross of late.

Scott looked at the satellite images on his computer screen. If he could get the property for a good price, it would be ideal for his needs. There already a medium sized two story brick home on the property. It appeared to be equipped with solar and wind power, yet had power lines going to the house as well. Scott assumed that the solar and wind was just a secondary source of power to help lower electricity bills, or to provide continuous power in the event of an occasional outage.

There were other things Scott saw that he liked as well. The biggest was that there were huge, two hundred foot high power lines that ran along the eastern border of the land. These were the same power lines that snaked south to San Antonio, and ran past the back of his current residence. It was seventy miles by his rough reckoning, but it was a critical connection. It meant that he could get his sons safely from one place to another if he had to, without traveling on any public roads.

On the northwest corner of the land was a stream that ran down from the mountains of Kerrville. Besides the well, a good secondary source of drinking water. And a water source that could be diverted to sustain a small pond on the property. A private pond that could be stocked with catfish and perch and crawfish.

He got out of Google Earth and logged onto a website for North San Antonio Equipment Company. He had a good friend who worked there, who'd give him a good deal on whatever used equipment they had available.

He settled on a used Bobcat earth mover. It was rather small, and the bucket on the front would only carry two cubic yards of dirt at a time. But it would go anywhere, and would be enough to dig out a hole thirty feet deep and half an acre across for his stock pond.

He liked the Bobcat's flexibility. For another eight hundred bucks, he could purchase a tree cutting attachment that would enable him to clear three acres of land to grow crops. Another seven hundred dollars and he'd own an auger attachment that would enable him to drill holes for fence posts. That would come in handy when he built his compound and put a ten foot high steel fence around it.

Lastly, he found a Ford 100 Farm-All tractor, two years old but with only three hundred hours on the engine. If he took good care of it, it would last at least twenty years.

Both the Bobcat and the tractor had diesel engines, which was essential to his needs. Diesel had a longer shelf life than gasoline, was more efficient, and was much safer. A bullet or a stray spark wouldn't make it go boom like gasoline.

Scott turned off his computer feeling good. If all went well, by the end of the week he'd not only have a deal in the works for his doomsday compound, but he'd also have a good start on stocking it with the equipment he'd need to ensure the survival of his family.

He heard the front door slam and looked at the clock above his desk. Four fifteen. His youngest son was right on time.

Zachary stuck his head around the corner of the door to Scott's office.

"Hi, Dad."

"Hello, son. How was school?"

"Yeah, well, you know… school is school. The only thing that ever changes is how much I hate it from one day to the next."

"Well, soon you'll be in high school, and everything will change. That'll be one of the happiest times in your life. You'll find a girlfriend and form friendships that will last you the rest of your life."

"I hope so, Dad. None of the girls in middle school are worth having. They're all either ugly, or they're dumber than dirt. I hope they get better in high school. What's for dinner?"

"Chicken spaghetti. Should be done in half an hour or so. Right around the time your brother gets home."

# -4-

It was exactly five o'clock when Zachary's older brother Jordan pulled into the driveway and came stomping into the house.

"Hey, son. How's stuff and things?"

"Hi Dad. If I live to be a thousand years old, I'll never understand women!"

Scott chuckled. "You're seventeen years old. You haven't even dated any women yet. What did Sara do this time?"

"She said she doesn't want to go to the dance tomorrow night after all. She said she was cramping today and that she thinks she's starting her..."

Scott cut him off. "Whoa, there, too much information. You don't think she has a right to cancel if she's not feeling well?"

"No, Dad, it's not that, it's just that... I was looking forward to this dance. I bought new clothes and washed my car and everything."

"Let me tell you something, son. There will be other dances. Lots of them. And you'll have other disappointments. In the grand scheme of things this is just a small pimple on the big ole butt of life."

Jordan looked at his father like he was insane. Then they both broke up laughing.

"A pimple on the butt of life? Are you serious?"

"My point is there will be other dances. If you care about Sara, give her a break. Women are sensitive about those kinds of things. Just be sensitive to her and tell her it's okay, you'll just do something else when she's feeling better. You can always wear those new clothes on another occasion. And your car needed to be washed anyway."

"Yeah, I guess so."

"Now, let's eat. Dinner is ready."

Scott purposely didn't tell his sons about the new property he wanted to buy, or his suspicion that every convenience in their modern world might soon be a thing of the past. He planned to keep them in the dark as long as possible, for a couple of reasons. First of all, he didn't want to worry them unnecessarily. Second, his family's survival would depend to a large degree on the level of security they could maintain. Both of his sons had a lot of friends, and neither could keep a secret. If word got out that when the stuff hit the fan, there was a safe place to go, everything Scott worked for would be in jeopardy.

So for the time being, it would be his little secret.

It helped that he was the owner of his self-storage units instead of the manager. He had an office in the largest of the facilities, but it was mostly so he had a comfortable place to hang out when he wanted to drop in and check up on things. He only went in a couple or three times a week, and then he didn't stay long.

His situation was ideal, really, for doing what he planned to do over the next few months. No one would be surprised if he didn't come around for days or even weeks at a time. It would give him plenty of time to spend his days at the compound.

After dinner he was back on his computer, doing research on a variety of things. He copied page after page of internet files into a single file folder on his computer's desktop. The folder was entitled "Doomsday File."

He researched the best varieties of wheat and corn to plant outside the compound, based on average rainfall and temperatures. Then he copied the information into his file.

He researched the basics of farming… how to plant, when to plant, how to harvest, and how to combat pests, weeds and drought. That information, as well, went into his file.

He researched the basics of ranching also. How to maintain and breed a small herd of cattle. A small herd of pigs. A small flock of chickens. A small colony of rabbits.

By the time his eyes grew heavy and he logged off his computer, his Doomsday File was already stuffed with over a hundred pages of helpful information. It would grow into many hundreds of pages in the months ahead.

At some point he would start printing everything out. His plan was to put everything in binders to leave behind for his sons to use after he was gone. In the meantime, if his doomsday happened – *when it happened* – he'd train his boys in as many things as he could. The binders would serve as a backup to refresh their memories.

Scott went to bed that night with his mind still racing. On his bedside table was a small notepad, on which he scribbled things periodically during the night. More things to buy, more things to research.

Survival plans.

He was going to be a busy man indeed in the months ahead.

## -5-

It was a beautiful morning for a drive. The traffic was light, the sun was shining, and it was shaping up to be a glorious day.

Scott drove his Expedition up Interstate 10 West to exit 484, then went a mile north to an unnamed gravel road. As promised on the realtor's web site, there were two orange plastic flags tied to a mesquite tree to mark the road.

The gravel road itself appeared to be well maintained. It was flat and smooth, and just wide enough to get pieces of heavy equipment in, so long as oncoming traffic was held up on the other end. He made a mental note to install a "Private Road" sign at the turnoff, just to keep out the curious.

He pulled up to the Ryan place just a few minutes after Joyce Allen, and met her at the doorway of the main house.

He smiled when he first saw her. She was nothing like he envisioned after talking to her on the phone. Tall, thin, and bleached blonde, just like most of the occasional girlfriends he'd had over the years.

He was much better at reading women in person than he was at guessing what they looked like by the sound of their voices, though. He could tell by the way she looked him up and down as he walked toward the house. She was definitely interested too.

She held out her hand for his. Hers was soft, and warm, and limp. That was good. It meant she recognized his strength and would be submissive to him. Scott liked submissive women. They were more willing to do the things he enjoyed the most.

Joyce, too, noticed the firmness of his handshake. She was pleased as well. She liked strong men who took charge, and she tried hard to please them. Perhaps this would be the man who'd finally free her from her nine to five.

But no, not yet. She shook that thought out of her mind. She had a sale to make. After the sale was made, she'd let her mind entertain other thoughts. When it came to selling real estate, Joyce was all business.

"This is the main house. Four bedrooms, two and a half baths, a partially finished basement. Overall, it's 2,885 feet of comfort."

Scott was impressed. It was newer than he expected, and in excellent shape. He expected a fixer upper, but this place was ready to move into. Still, he wouldn't show his interest in hopes of negotiating a better deal.

"How come the family is selling it?"

"The old man lived here by himself, but none of his children wanted to take it over. They said it was too far from the city. He apparently grew up on a farm and enjoyed an isolated existence. They didn't. So when he died, none of the children wanted the house. They decided by mutual agreement to sell it and split the money between them."

Scott looked around and held a poker face, although he really liked what he saw. Sturdy, thick walls, copper plumbing, double paned windows and doors. A fireplace on the first floor and another in the master bedroom upstairs.

"On the satellite photos I saw on Google Earth, I thought I saw solar panels on the roof and a small wind turbine out back. Does that mean it's energy self sufficient?"

"Oh, yes. Mr. Ryan's children told me that he hated to pay utility bills. The solar panels generate up to two kilowatts per hour on a sunny day. The turbine generates up to four kilowatts an hour when the wind is blowing at five miles an hour or greater. I have a wind survey that says the prevailing winds blow at that rate an average of four hours a day. It does have city power from Junction, but only as a backup. The family said they've only had to use it when the other systems were down for maintenance, or occasionally in the dead of winter."

"Yes, I'd like to see that, if you don't mind. Do you have a water survey as well?"

"Yes, sir. The wind turbine doubles as a water well pump. You've got a 4,000 gallon water tank behind the house that will stay constantly full. I'll have to double check the water survey, but I think it rates the water table as sufficient to provide your residential needs for at least two hundred years.

"If you bring in horses or livestock, you've got a good sized stock tank on the property as well. A stream runs completely through the corner of the property and this is the last privately owned plot in the area. Everything south of here is federal land, owned by the United States government. That means you own the water rights to the stream and can use as much water from it as you choose to."

"Do you know the source of the stream?"

This man knows his stuff, Joyce thought. And she liked that. It meant he did his homework. And Scott liked that she knew the answers.

"Yes, sir. It breaks off the Llano River up north of here. And if your next question is, 'are there fish in it?' the answer would be yes. Perch and dollies."

Scott liked what he saw. And he wanted the property. Now all that was left was the negotiation.

"Would you pass my offer of a million dollars to the owners?"

"Certainly. I'll call them today and let you know what they say."

Joyce wasn't happy that her potential commission had dropped. But at least she had an offer on the place. And at a million dollars, her commission would still be substantial.

"Is there anything else you'd like to see, Mr. Harter?"

"Yes, please. The water and geologic surveys."

"Certainly. I've got them in the back of my car. I'll give them to you on our way out."

Joyce locked the front door and led Scott to the back of her Honda CRV. She opened up the hatchback, and then opened a large metal trunk.

Mark noticed that the inside of the trunk was lined with foam rubber.

As Joyce was leafing through file folders in the trunk, looking for the surveys, Scott remarked, "That looks an awful lot like a Foley box."

She stopped looking just long enough to eye him. His comment piqued her interest.

"Oh, here they are," she said, pulling out three folders. "And the wind survey as well." She handed them to him and then remarked, "You know about Foley boxes?"

"Oh, yes. I've been doing some research lately about sun spot activity and such. So that's what it is?"

She laughed and said, "Yes. I'm busted. That's exactly what it is. It's been in the back of my car since early 2012, when everybody was saying the world was going to end on December 21st. One of the theories was that it was going to be bombarded with solar flares. So I bought this old metal trunk and lined it in foam rubber, and kept a few things in it.

"Go ahead, you can laugh at me. All my friends did. They called me the 'doomsday prepper.'"

Mark smiled, but didn't laugh.

"On the contrary. I think it's very prudent to plan for something catastrophic that might happen in the future. What did you have in the box, if you don't mind me asking?"

"I had a spare car battery, ignition and starter solenoid. A spare ignition computer and fuse box with fuses. A two way radio and flashlights with several pairs of spare batteries. Things I'd need to get me to a safe place if my car got fried out in the middle of nowhere."

"And the two way radio was to contact your husband and tell him not to worry?"

"Oh, there is no husband. No, the two way radio would be to contact a couple of close girlfriends who were also preppers."

Scott's eyebrow went up when she mentioned that she was single. She noticed. Both filed away their information for later.

"I think it's very interesting, Mr. Harter, that you know what a Foley box is. Does that mean that you're a prepper too?"

"No. Well, at least I wasn't during the 2012 Mayan thing when the rest of the world was going nuts."

He caught himself, and said, "No offense."

She smiled and said, "None taken, Mr. Harter."

"Please, call me Scott. I didn't believe in the whole end of the world in December 2012 thing. But I have done some research on sun spot activity since then. And I believe it's only a matter of time before a major solar storm sends EMPs that are capable of doing great damage to the power grids. In fact, I think it's inevitable. If I were you, I'd hang onto this Foley box. Just in case."

"Well thank you… Scott. And thank you also for not thinking me looney, like my friends did."

"Oh, I don't think you're looney at all."

He smiled, and wondered… Then he came back to reality.

"I won't be home much the next couple of days, but I'll have my cell with me twenty four seven. Please let me know what the Ryan family thinks of my offer."

Joyce held out her hand for his, and once again appreciated his strong grip. She wondered what those hands might feel like exploring her body.

"Thank you again, Scott. I'll definitely be in touch."

# -6-

Scott sat at his desk and looked over the reports he'd gotten from Joyce. Water wasn't going to be a problem. Neither was electrical power. He had seen an unused room in the partially finished basement. It would be ideal for placing several industrial sized batteries for storing power. He'd looked at plans he found on line for a self-contained power system, and he planned to install one in the basement of the Ryan house.

His plan was simple. When the wind was blowing, the wind turbine generated more power than the house used. So with battery storage available, the excess could be stored for whenever the wind wasn't blowing. Likewise, on a bright sunny day, the solar panels generated more energy than the house needed. That excess power could also be stored in the batteries, for use at night and on cloudy days.

Scott planned to purchase a good sized diesel generator for backup, but according to his calculations, it would only be needed occasionally. When, say for example, there was no significant sunshine or wind for more than two days. By his estimates, that shouldn't happen more than a few times a year. And it would only be for short periods of time. A diesel generator would ensure uninterrupted power as long as his supply of diesel fuel held out. And he planned to stock a lot of it.

He got in his car and drove to the Hobby Lobby in the strip mall near his house. It took him awhile to find what he was looking for. But finally, on the bottom shelf of a kitchen nick-knack aisle, he found small tin boxes for holding oversized recipe cards. They were just the right size for holding a walkie talkie and eight AA batteries. He bought three of them, a large sheet of quarter inch thick rubber, a bottle of contact cement and a pair of scissors. And a Snickers bar at the register. Preparing for the end of civilization worked up a powerful hunger.

He got home and settled in at his dining room table just a few minutes before Zachary walked in the front door.

"Hi, Dad! What are you up to?"

"I'm making survival packs for you and your brother."

"Oh, okay. What's for dinner?" Zachary had stopped being surprised years before of his father's occasional odd habits. If he was at all curious about the "survival packs" he didn't let on.

"Call Papa John's and order a couple of pizzas, will you?"

Zachary didn't have to be told twice. His father was a passing cook. But Papa John's was so much better.

Scott carefully measured the inside of the small tin boxes he'd bought from Hobby Lobby. Then he cut the rubber and lined the inside of each box. Once pleased with the fit, he glued the rubber into place with contact cement.

Then he opened up a package of three Motorola 22-channel two way radios that he'd bought a few days before. He set each one on channel 5, and placed one in each of the boxes. Each radio needed four batteries to operate. He doubled that amount and put eight batteries in each box as well. Then he closed the lid. It was a perfect fit.

He pulled out a large Target shopping bag which contained three identical black backpacks. He placed a tin box within each of the bags. Then he took six bottles of drinking water from an open case behind him and placed two in each backpack. He added four granola bars from a package in the cupboard.

Lastly, he took a black sharpie and a 5" x 7" index card and sat down to write:

*Dear Zachary,*

*"Wherever you are when the power goes out and the cars all stop, take this backpack and make your way home immediately.*

*Move only in daylight. If you cannot make it home before dark, spend the night in an abandoned car. They will be everywhere. All the streets and freeways will be covered with them. Find one that is unlocked, crawl in and sleep there. The next morning continue on your way home.*

*Do not talk to anyone. You will not know who is friend and who is foe.*

*Place four batteries in the radio and turn it on. Do not let anyone see you do this. They might try to take it away from you. Leave it on channel 5 and call me when you can do so without being seen. The best way is to crawl inside an abandoned car and duck down.*

*When you get home I may or may not be there. If I am not, wait until I get there. If anyone tries to rob the house, do not resist them. Let them take whatever they want. I don't want you getting hurt trying to protect the house. The house is not worth your life.*

*I love you, Zachary. This will be hard, but we will get through it together."*

He made a second note, identical except that this one was made out for his oldest son Jordan. He placed one note in each of two backpacks and set them aside.

He was finishing up when Jordan walked into the house and said, "Hey, the pizza guy pulled up right behind me. All right, no Dad cooking tonight!" Zachary laughed and they high fived each other.

Scott handed Jordan two twenties and said, "You guys start without me, I'm in the middle of something. Jordan, let me borrow your car keys."

While his sons got into a lively debate at the dinner table about whether Canadian bacon and ham were the same thing, Scott went out to the garage. He rolled a brand new ten speed bicycle into the driveway, took the wheels off of it, and placed it into Jordan's trunk. Then he placed the wheels on top of it. He took the back pack he prepared for Jordan and shoved it into the back part of the trunk, where it would be out of the way.

Then he went back into the house.

"You guys finished yet?"

Zachary had pizza sauce on his chin. He wasn't the neatest of eaters.

"Nope. Not yet."

"Well, then, grab another piece and come outside. I have something to show you."

Each of the boys grabbed a slice of pizza for the trip and followed Scott out into the driveway.

Jordan looked inside the trunk of his car and saw the new bicycle and backpack.

"Hey, cool, but why…"

"Okay, boys, I want you to listen closely, this is important."

Jordan and Zachary sensed a seriousness in Scott's voice and gave him their undivided attention.

"You guys know I am not the kind of person who freaks out unnecessarily. But I have a very good reason to believe that a major change is coming to the earth sometime in the next year or two. I don't know exactly when. It could be five minutes from now, or next year, or the year after that. But I am certain it is going to happen. At some point, there will be a major solar storm on the surface of the sun. It will produce a series of solar flares the likes we haven't seen in our lifetimes. In fact, these will be greater than any we've experienced since man started developing machines.

"Do you remember a couple of months ago, when there were some solar flares that disrupted the communications satellites, and our cell phones kept dropping calls and the TV picture kept going out?"

The boys looked at each other and shook their heads.

"It'll be like that, only a thousand times more powerful. Instead of just messing with our communications satellites, the massive storm will send electric static waves that will bombard the earth. They won't do any damage to humans, but they will be strong enough to short out anything that has a battery, or anything that had a circuit board which can be short circuited. That means no cars will work, no computers, no electronics. Nothing you plug into a wall or put batteries into will work anymore."

He took out the small metal box from Jordan's backpack.

"There is, however, one way to protect things from being destroyed. I made this based on what scientists call a 'Foley cage.' Somebody named Foley invented a concept whereby electronics were stored within a metal container, but were insulated from direct contact with the container. The idea is that when solar flares send electromagnetic pulses, or EMPs, toward the earth, they will hit the box and run around its surface. But the electronics inside are insulated from the EMPs. Therefore they are protected and can still be used."

He opened up the box so the boys could see the rubber insulation, and took out the radio.

"As I said, I don't know when it's going to happen. It could happen while we're at home. That would be the best thing. But it might happen while you're at school, or while you're en route.

"Jordan, if you're at school and all the lights go out, try to call me. If the lights at school don't work, and your cell phone doesn't work, and none of your friends' phones work either, then it'll be time. When you go out to your car, you'll notice cars on the streets in front of the school have all died.

"There will be people getting out of their cars and looking under their hoods and scratching their heads, trying to figure out why everybody's cars all died at the same time.

"When that happens, leave all your books behind. You won't need them anymore. Take this bike out of your trunk and put the wheels on it. It's a racing bike. The wheels have thumbnuts so they can be installed quickly without wrenches. Put the wheels on the bike, put your backpack on, and ride home as quickly as possible.

"People will try to flag you down, or ask you to get help. Do not stop. They may be friendly, or they may want to take your bike. People will be desperate and scared. Keep moving.

"If someone does succeed in taking your bike, don't put up a fight. Give it up without getting yourself hurt. Then walk home. Your school is just over twelve miles from home. I clocked it. You should be able to make it home in one day. If for some reason you can't, find one of the cars on the road that is unlocked and sleep there for the night.

"At some point, I want you to duck behind a building or some trees and take the radio out of the backpack. Put the batteries in it and turn it on, and then call me to tell me you're on your way and when I can expect you. Do you understand?"

Jordan's lip quivered, but he nodded his head yes. Scott turned to his younger son.

"Zachary, the same applies for you, but without the bike. Your school is only six miles away. You can make it in one day. You'll have to take this backpack with you every day, but there is still room in it for your books and such. There are two bottles of water and some granola bars for each of you if you get hungry or thirsty on the way.

"Zach, if you're at school when everything goes out, walk out of school and head home. If any of the teachers try to stop you and say it's just a power outage, ignore them. Walk right past them and out the door. Your life will depend on it. The same thing applies if the bus dies on the way to or from school. You'll know it's happened because all of the other vehicles on the road will die too at the same time. And your cell phone won't work.

"I don't want either of you to worry or be scared. Once we meet here, I've got a safe place for us to go, and I will protect a vehicle that will get us there."

Zachary thought of his mother, who lived with her boyfriend a couple of miles away.

"What about Mom?"

"I will talk to your mother. She is very stubborn, but I will tell her if she can get here within a few hours of the blackout we will take her with us."

"Dad, I'm scared."

"That's why I'm telling you all of this, son. I know it's a lot to absorb, and it's a scary thought. But me telling you this is a good thing. You can put your mind at ease, knowing that while the rest of the city is panicking and going into chaos mode, that we'll have a safe place to go, and we'll survive while many others won't. All you have to do is make it home. I've got everything covered after that."

Scott went to sleep that night wondering if he'd done the right thing by telling his boys. They were likely to mention it to some of their friends, and it might open them up to ridicule. They might be called crazy.

But no, he finally decided he needed to tell them. Mostly because they had a right to know that something that would affect them to such a great degree was likely to happen soon. Also, if they were caught by surprise, they might panic. If it happened while they were in school, they might go to the home of a friend who lived close to the school. And while they would surely be safe there, without telephones they'd have no way to tell Scott where they were.

Now he just had to figure out a way to tell their mother without her freaking out.

## -7-

A couple of weeks after he closed on the old Ryan place, Scott was there, in the main house, unloading a truck full of furniture and dishes from one of his abandoned storage lockers. There was a knock on the door.

He opened it up to find Joyce, carrying a house plant and bottle of wine.

Scott wasn't surprised. At the closing, she kept catching his eye. It was obvious she was interested. And, Scott had to admit to himself, he was too.

"Hi. I hope this isn't too much of a bother. I just wanted to drop off a housewarming gift, and..."

She left it at that, afraid to go further.

But Scott wasn't quite so shy.

"I hate to drink alone. I'll accept your generous gift, but only if you stick around long enough to share it with me."

She smiled a warm smile. She was quite attractive, Scott had decided. And definitely his type.

"Why, thank you, Mr. Harter. I'd love to, but... I'm afraid the wine isn't chilled."

"First of all, no one calls me Mr. Harter. Mr. Harter sounds like a stuffy old codger. Call me Scott, please. And the wine isn't a problem. I have a friend who's a wine snob from Europe. He insists that only American fools chill their wine before drinking it. He insists that wine and beer taste better at room temperature. Let's find out. And while we're finding out, we can get to know each other."

It was her turn to smile. She'd already decided she wanted to get to know him a lot better.

"Okay, but you'll have to keep an eye on me to make sure I don't drink so much that I can't drive home."

Scott's expression told her he was thinking the same thing she was.

He took the bottle out of the gift bag and read the label. An Eifel spatlase. She had good taste in wine.

"Have you been to the Eifel region?

"No, I've actually never left the States. An old friend got me hooked on German wines several years ago."

She looked around.

"I was expecting to see your boys, Scott. You said you had two of them?"

He saw right through her. She was fishing.

"Yes, but you won't see them today, I'm afraid. They are with their mother this weekend."

"But you have full-time custody? Pardon me if it sounds like I'm prying, but that's unusual in Texas. For a father to have custody, I mean."

"Oh, I don't mind. It's no secret. Linda had some problems about the time we were going through our divorce. She gave me custody without a fight because she knew they were safer with me. And because she had her own personal demons to fight, and she couldn't do that while raising the boys. She's been clean and sober for five years now, and she's changed her bad habits. So even though I have custody, we have a very liberal visitation arrangement. And she and I are still good friends."

"It's nice when you can end things amicably. I wish my own marriage had ended as well. But he's gone forever, and I haven't seen him for years. So that's all water under the bridge, I suppose."

"Do you have any children, Joyce?"

"No, not me. I always assumed it was Ron. My ex. But then after we divorced I got tested. I'm unable to. But that's okay. I'm too much of a space cadet to have kids. I'd probably leave them at the supermarket by accident or something. That's how scatterbrained I am."

"Oh, I doubt that. You strike me as a woman with a great head on your shoulders, who knows exactly what she wants and how to get it."

He smiled and she blushed. It was at that point she realized that all pretense was gone. He knew she wanted him, and his warm smile told her he was more than willing. They'd just dance around the subject a bit more. Play the waiting game. But before the night was over she'd be sharing his bed. She was sure of it.

Scott found a couple of wine glasses in one of the boxes and washed and dried them. He poured them each a glass. This time he abandoned his easy chair and sat down on the couch beside her. He liked the way she smelled.

Two hours later the bottle of wine was down to its last drops, and Joyce was feeling no pain. Scott was certain he could have his way with her, but was too much of a gentleman to take advantage of her. So he offered her a way out.

"If you'd like, I can run you home and pick you up again tomorrow. Or, if you'd like, I can put you up in the guest room. I just stocked the bathroom with a bunch of girly stuff. They may not be the brands you're used to, but I'm confident you'll have everything you need."

She laughed.

"First of all, 'girly stuff?' You make me smile, Scott Harter. And second of all," she said as she leaned over and kissed him, "don't forget I was the one who showed you this place. I've been in the master bedroom. And it's much more to my liking."

He kissed her back. Then he got up and said, "Well, then. It's a chilly night, and the master bedroom is a bit drafty. How about I get a nice fire going in there?"

"Great idea. While you're doing that, I'm going to make use of your shower. And I'll leave the door cracked in case you care to join me."

He smiled at the thought.

"Well, dear lady, I just might do that."

The next morning Scott arose before Joyce and fixed her breakfast.

She walked into the kitchen with her hair a mess, but she didn't care. The smile on her face told him she'd had a good time.

"Hey, cowboy. I was hoping for another round this morning, but I smelled the bacon and now I'm conflicted."

He laughed.

"We can do both. But if we eat first we'll have more energy to do the other. How do you like your eggs?"

She laughed.

"I just thought of an old joke. A man asks a woman how she likes her eggs and she says, 'fertilized.'"

Then she turned red.

"I'm sorry. That was just a bit naughty, wasn't it?"

Scott said with a chuckle, "Listen at you. You're standing in my kitchen wearing nothing but a smile, and you're worried about being naughty. I'd say you're way past naughty, my dear."

"Good point, cowboy. And I like my eggs scrambled, with cheese if you have some."

"I do indeed. Sit right there and look beautiful while I finish this up. Or you can make us some coffee. Have you used a Keurig before?"

"Oh, yes. I can't live without mine."

"Good. Look in the second door on the right for the Keurig cups. I'd like some traditional roast, if you don't mind."

She said, "It figures," but didn't elaborate.

As she sipped her coffee she studied him, standing in front of the stove in a pair of light blue boxers. She guessed they were the same age, give or take a couple of years. He aged well, and was in much better shape than most men his age. He still had his hair and all his teeth, and had some good grooming habits. She'd dated some real pigs in recent years, so this was a nice change.

"Scott, can I ask you a personal question?"

"Sure."

"A few weeks ago, when we met out here for the first time, you commented on the box I have in my trunk. The one where I keep my files. You knew what a Foley cage was and what it was used for. You mentioned something about solar flares and EMPs. You said it was just a matter of time. Do you think it's going to be soon?"

"I don't know for sure. I mean who can say? I did some research on the Mayans and the things they were able to do without what we consider modern technology. And I was amazed. And I did some research on a professor who claimed to have translated some of the Mayan hieroglyphics.

He believed that 2012 opened a window of great risk for solar storms and EMPs. He also believed very strongly that within just a few years solar storms would zap us back to the stone age."

Joyce smiled. "Prepper. That's what my friends called me when they found out I was preparing for something bad to happen on December 21st, 2012. They said it with disdain, like they were mocking me. When nothing happened they ridiculed me. But I never got rid of my extra food stores. I just feel something coming. I can't explain it. But I am positive something is going to happen. Sooner than later. Perhaps you're right. Maybe the Mayans were right. Maybe we were right. For preparing for the end of the world."

Scott hadn't had any plans to tell her about the old professor's notes and his own research. But he liked this woman, and thought there was a good chance they'd grow closer. And it couldn't hurt, after all.

So after he scooped their bacon, eggs and toast onto their plates, he sat down across from her and looked across the table into her eyes.

"As a matter of fact, let me tell you why I bought this place…"

# -8-

The following Tuesday morning Scott was back at the compound, awaiting a truck that was going to deliver a load of angle iron and sheet metal roofing panels. They told him they'd be there sometime around noon, so he had some time to kill. He decided he'd spend it on his new Bobcat, clearing a section of land for planting crops.

He climbed aboard the Bobcat and was reaching for the ignition when his cell rang.

The caller ID said Linda, and he thought for a brief moment about ignoring it. But he had to fill her in sooner or later, and it was probably better to do it on the phone than in person.

Linda was the mother of his sons. They were sweethearts in school together, but she was never quite on his maturity level. She'd had a rough life, both during and after their marriage, with alcohol and drugs guiding her into a long series of bad decisions. She was clean and sober now, but still not the best decision maker.

"Hello."

"Hi, Scott. How are you?"

"I'm fine, Linda. How are you doing?"

"I'm good. I just wanted to let you know that Zach left a book here this past weekend. It looks like it's from the school library. If I know Zach, it's probably past due. How about if I drop it off sometime this evening?"

"Sure. Not a problem, and thanks. If it's a burden I can swing by your office on my way home."

"Well, that's the thing. I quit my job a couple of days ago, and I'm home. I have a new job lined up this time. I'm learning that much at least. But I don't start until Monday, so I'm just chillin' at the crib, as the boys say these days."

"Is Glen there?"

"No, he went fishing with his buddies. He won't be back for a couple of days."

"Well, I'll tell you what. I'm kinda tied up right now. How about if I drop by your house on my way home this afternoon. I'll pick up the book and save you a trip. There's something I want to talk to you about anyway, and that'll give us a chance to talk without the boys interrupting us."

"Okay. Sounds good. I'll see you this afternoon."

Scott cranked up the Bobcat. He liked the way it handled. It was diesel driven and turned on a dime. And it had more than enough power to do everything he needed.

He'd spent half an hour installing a tree pulling attachment onto the front of the machine. It was essentially a set of hydraulic jaws that could be closed around a tree trunk. If the trunk was less than five inches thick, it could snap it in half like a twig.

That wasn't Scott's plan, though. With a little less pressure on the jaws, Scott could grab small trees and simply rock them back and forth. He had identified a section of land on his new spread about the size and shape of two football fields laid side by side. A little over two acres, he figured. It was relatively flat, and close enough to the well to be easily irrigated when rain was scarce.

The problem was, it needed to be cleared. It was covered with sixty or seventy mesquite trees.

Scott's original plan was to cut down the trees, cut them into firewood, and use them as emergency fuel should the need ever arise. But then he had a better idea.

He knew that mesquite trees had very shallow root systems. And their root systems were very brittle. He knew that it would be easier to pull each tree out of the ground, roots and all, than to cut it down. Plus, pulling them out of the ground would alleviate the problem of having to go back later and removing the stumps.

Scott knew also that because mesquite trees were covered with savage thorns an inch long, they would make an excellent natural barrier to help keep out prowlers.

To test his plan, he wrapped the jaws of his Bobcat around the six inch trunk of an old mesquite. Instead of trying to cut it, though, he merely pushed it forward a foot or two. Then he pulled it back. He did this a couple of more times and could almost feel the tree giving up. Then he merely lifted up the jaw attachment, and the tree came out of the ground. Some of the root system was left behind, but that wasn't a problem. Once the section of land was cleared, Scott would plow it under. The roots would be chopped to pieces and would degrade into fertilizer.

He used the Bobcat to carry the tree to the gravel road which served as a driveway to his compound. He drove backwards, because the tree blocked his forward view, and selected a spot next to the gravel road about one hundred yards from the house.

Then he very carefully placed the mesquite tree on the ground, opened the jaws, and shoved it forward. It fell perfectly into place.

The mesquite tree's inch long thorns were as hard as nails. The thorns are quite painful, and notorious for causing serious infections. It was Mother Nature's best effort at making a barbed wire fence.

With the tree lying on the ground, with its trunk inside the compound and pointing toward the house, intruders on foot would have the formidable challenge of having to crawl through the tree branches. And while one tree wouldn't keep out a determined intruder, a long line of them, completely surrounding the perimeter of the property, just might.

And if it didn't keep them out, it would damn sure slow them down. And cause them some pain.

Scott suspected that the trees would also be effective in stopping vehicle traffic. Mesquite thorns have been known to flatten tires. And the tree trunks, laying low to the ground, would dig into the dirt and provide some good resistance to a vehicle pushing against them.

Hopefully that wouldn't be a problem, of course. The only vehicles that would be running after the EMP storm would belong to those who had planned ahead and protected the vehicles. And anyone with enough sense to do that would have their pick of targets to get food from. Softer targets than Scott's compound, anyway.

He uprooted about twenty trees, placing them carefully in a line with the first tree, so that they overlapped and there was no safe passage between them. He decided to take a short break at the same time his delivery truck came barreling down the road.

Scott liked that the road was made of caliche and gravel, instead of pavement. He could see the cloud of dust rising over the trees in the distance long before he saw the truck. Another effective tool against intruders and marauders.

Luckily for Scott, the truck came with a three-wheeled forklift attached to the back. He could have offloaded it with his Bobcat, but that would have meant taking the tree attachment off the front and installing the forklift tines. Only a twenty minute job, but then he'd have to spend another twenty minutes after the truck left to take the tines back off again. The trucker bringing his own lift just made things easier.

"Howdy, partner!" The trucker was a jovial sort. "Where abouts you want this stuff?"

Scott instructed the driver to drop his load on the south side of the house. That's where he'd start building his ten foot privacy fence. He'd start there and just move the materials around with him as he went.

His plan was to start at the front of the house. On the southwest corner, he'd plant a metal post, and then run a series of metal posts every ten feet for a hundred yards. Then he'd turn north and continue the process. When he finished, he'd have a ten foot tall steel fence measuring two hundred yards wide and a hundred yards long. It would be large enough to grow a large fruit and vegetable garden, a small orchard of fruit trees, and would provide corrals and pens for various livestock.

It wouldn't be cheap, of course. But he'd learned how to weld as a welder's apprentice after high school. He'd maintained his certification all the years since, so that he could do a lot of the repairs himself at his storage facilities and save some money. He could spot weld a broken overhead door in just a few minutes and save several hundred dollars each time he didn't have to call in a repairman. And, by God, if he could do that, then he could damn well install a privacy fence.

When he did the mortgage paperwork for the property, he'd had the bank throw in an additional hundred thousand dollars for a home improvement loan. That would cover all the materials for the privacy fence, as well as additional motors and electronic components for the well pumps, wind turbine and solar panel console. All of those, of course, would be stored in a garage sized Foley cage he planned to build when he wasn't building the fence. It was a good thing he didn't really have to go into work everyday. There was quite enough to keep him busy at the compound.

## -9-

Scott looked at his watch. It was a quarter past five. Both boys would be home from school by now. He took his cell out of his pocket and called home.

"Hey, Jordan, how'd your day go?"

"Oh heck, Dad. Don't even ask!"

"Girl problems again?"

"Good guess."

"Get used to it son. It never gets any easier. I'm no closer to figuring women out than I was at your age." He chuckled.

"You gonna be home anytime soon, Dad? Or do you want me to start dinner?"

"Ask your brother if he's hungry. I'm going to stop and visit with your mother for a few minutes and pick up Zach's library book. It'll be a couple of hours before I get home. If y'all want to eat before then, go ahead. If you can wait, let me know. I'll stop by Taco Cabana and get something to go."

Scott held the line for a few seconds until his oldest son came back.

"Zach says he'd rather have Taco Cabana than anything I can cook."

"Yeah, that's what I thought. Okay, I'll be there in a couple of hours."

He climbed into his truck for the forty five minute drive to Linda's house, surprised at how stiff his muscles were. It dawned on him then that he wasn't getting any younger. He wasn't quite feeling his age, not yet. But in the years ahead it would be comforting knowing that he'd have two sturdy boys to help him with the heavy work. And they were both good boys. He'd made sure of that. They'd work all day without complaint. Pretty rare for most kids their age.

A bit later he pulled up in front of Linda's house. He was glad to see that Glen's raggedy ass truck wasn't in the driveway. It wasn't that he didn't like Glen, he told himself. It was just that Linda could have done much better than a man who went from job to job, only working long enough to make a few paychecks. Then he'd find a reason to quit. The manager had it in for him. Or the rules were too strict. Or they didn't recognize his potential. Or they screwed him out of a promotion. Then he'd lay on the couch for weeks at a time until the bills backed up and Linda started begging him to go back to work.

Linda had had her own problems, sure. But they were in the past. She'd come a long way. She certainly didn't need a dirt bag like Glen dragging her down.

Then Scott shook it out of his system. Wasn't his business. Except that maybe it was.

Linda answered the door and gave Scott a warm smile that he'd never really gotten over despite all the bad that had happened between them over the years.

"Come on in, Scott. Can I get you a beer?"

"Sure, why not?"

She came back from the kitchen with a bottle of Bud Light for him and a can of Diet Coke for herself. That was a good sign. If she'd been drinking again she'd had taken the opportunity to get herself a beer as well.

They made a little bit of small talk, but Scott was careful not to let it get out of hand. He wanted to get home to the boys, and needed to get the important stuff out of the way.

"I've got something serious I need to talk to you about. But first, I need to tell you that there's a good chance you'll think I'm crazy."

"Oh, please, Scott. Give me a little bit of credit. I've never thought you crazy. You're the most level headed man I've known in a long time. Probably my entire life."

"Good. That'll make it a little bit easier."

She leaned forward and listened intently. She hadn't seen him so tense in a very long time.

"You remember in the months leading up to December, 2012, how the whole country was freaking out and saying the world was going to end?"

She hesitated at the implication and then slowly said, "Yes..."

"I have come to believe that there was some validity in that after all. I mean, I've found a lot of material that seems to indicate the Mayans never said the world was going to end that day. What they actually said was that date would begin a time when the world was in for a time of great adversity and tribulation. The window would open, at that time, of a period which would cause a major change in how man lived."

Linda was puzzled.

"What are you saying?"

"I believe that sometime in the near future, within the next couple or three years, that the sun will have a series of very vicious solar storms. I believe they will be so powerful that they will bombard the earth with what scientists call electro-magnetic pulses, or EMPs. And that they will be so powerful that nothing electrical or electronic, including our vehicles, will work anymore."

"Ever?"

"Ever. Or at least until they are all rebuilt, with new parts. But they won't have the electricity to power the machinery to make the replacement parts. So yes. You might as well say forever."

She couldn't quite wrap her head around the concept.

"So... what will happen to people? Will we survive?"

"Mankind will go back to the way they lived before the industrial age. Back in the 1800s. Before electricity and cars were invented. There will be no more shopping at the local grocery store. Man will have to learn to grow his food. Or to kill it. And for many who don't know how to do either, there's a third option. They'll steal it."

"Oh, my God! Is there anything we can do to prevent it from happening?"

"No. There is no way to stop it. But there are ways to protect a limited amount of equipment from getting ruined. It's not easy. And it's not cheap. But it's possible to save enough equipment, and enough electricity, to power and run on a small scale. In a safe place that is well hidden. People won't try to steal it if they don't know it exists."

"Is that why you bought that land up there in the middle of nowhere?"

"Yes. That's exactly why. I won't be going in to work much over the next few months. They can get by without me.

What I will be doing is getting the place ready, so that when the time comes it'll be a safe place to go."

Linda hesitated, as though afraid to ask the question.

"Safe... for who?"

Scott suddenly felt pity, and maybe a bit of deeply buried love, for her.

"Don't worry. I wouldn't leave you out. We have too much history. And the boys wouldn't want to go on without you."

She sighed deeply. It occurred to Scott at that moment that she surely regretted what her life had become and wanted things to be the way they used to be. When she and Scott were married and he took care of her and covered for her addictions.

But they both knew there had been way too much water under that bridge to go back.

"Here's the thing. When the time comes, I want you to make your way to my house. I had a spare house key made for you. Here it is. Put it on your key ring with the rest of your keys, and don't tell Glen what it's for. I don't trust him. You might, but I don't."

He pressed the key into her hand. She took the opportunity to grasp his hand and to hold it for a moment. Then he drew away.

"When it happens, make your way to my house. In my office, in the file drawer, you'll find a folder with your name on it. You'll have to open the window blinds, because the power will be out. But you can find it.

"Once you find the folder, open it up and follow the instructions. It'll tell you everything you need to do to protect yourself, and to tell me that you're ready. And then I will come for you. I'll bring you to the compound and you'll be safe."

She hesitated again. She was almost afraid of the likely answer to her next question.

"Scott... what about Glen?"

He took a deep breath before answering.

"Look. I don't like or trust Glen. You know that. But I realize that he is the man in your life now, and it's not my place to try to tell you who to be with.

"If you want to bring Glen with you, then bring him. However, he has to realize that running the compound will take a lot of work on everybody's part. There will be crops to raise, livestock to care for, chores to do. Guard duty for the men. It won't be a vacation resort. The only thing Glen knows about work is how to avoid it."

She winced. Scott's words hit too close for comfort.

He went on.

"If you want to bring him along, that's your business. But if he refuses to carry his share of the load, he will become a chain around everybody's neck. And I swear to God, I will shoot him in the head and bury him up there."

"You can't be serious."

Then she looked in his eyes and knew he was.

"Yes, I am, and here's why. If he is not carrying his load, then he will be an unnecessary drain on our resources. He will eat our food and drink our water without helping to replenish it. We cannot just banish him or kick him out. He'd gather up his buddies and tell them that we have livestock, and crops, and a secure compound with hot water and electricity.

"And then he and his friends would try to take over the compound. And since Glen had been on the inside, he'd know the security system. He'd know the weak spots.

"And do not kid yourself, Linda. If it gets to that point, he won't come in asking nicely if he can steal everything we have. He'll come in with guns blazing. And if you get shot, or the boys get shot, he won't give a diddly damn. Because men like Glen only care about themselves. I'm surprised that after all this time you can't see him for the user he is.

"But again, that's none of my business."

She was suddenly ashamed. Ashamed for having put herself in such a bad spot that she had to settle for a man like Glen to give her the affection and attention she craved. And she knew Scott was right. Glen took a hell of a lot more than he gave.

Scott saw the sadness on her face. This time he took hold of her hands, and looked into her moistening eyes.

"Look, this might hurt you. And if it does, I'm sorry. But you need to make a decision, ahead of time, whether to bring him with you. If you bring him, I will give him the benefit of the doubt. Maybe he'll step up. Just understand what will happen if he doesn't."

"How will I know when it happens?"

Scott couldn't help but laugh.

"It'll be hard not to notice. The power will go out. For everybody. It'll be like a city wide blackout. Except that your cell phone won't work either. Nobody's will. And every car, every truck, will stop dead in its tracks. Airplanes will fall from the sky. It will become deathly quiet. Everyone will be in the streets, trying to figure out what's happening. Asking when the power will come back on.

"And it won't. Not ever again."

She started to cry. Against his better judgment he held her.

"Keep a bicycle handy. In fact, get a second bike. One you can keep in your trunk. I'll help you pick out one that you can put the wheels on easily without tools.

"And when everything goes off, ride that bike as fast as you can to my house. If you can't get to your bike, then walk. Run if you can. Just get there.

"I've clocked it. Your house is exactly nine miles from mine. I know it's a long way, but you can make it in less than two hours by bike. You can walk there in half a day. If you get there quickly enough, you may catch the boys and I before I take them to the compound.

"If not, find the folder with your name on it. It will tell you everything you need to do. And I'll come back for you, I promise."

"Scott, I've got to ask you this. I suspect I already know the answer. And it terrifies me. But if I don't ask you I will spend the rest of my life kicking myself. And I've got to know.

"Once this thing happens, once we are together with the boys up at your compound, and if I leave Glen behind, is there…"

Her voice broke.

Scott knew her question was difficult, and he spared her the pain of having to ask it. At the same time, though, he didn't want to lead her on or let her get the wrong idea.

"I'm going to invite someone else to the compound. Another woman. Mostly because she is experienced in survival techniques and will be a helpful addition to our group. But I'd be lying if I told you I didn't feel some attraction to her."

"I see."

"Linda, I'm not saying that what you are asking… were getting ready to ask… is not possible. At this point I don't know what may happen. And at this point it doesn't really matter. Let's just focus on getting everyone safely there, and then let everything else fall where it may."

He rose and she followed him to the door. She hugged him goodbye.

He started to walk out the door, and she stopped him.

"Scott…"

"Yes?"

"Thank you… for caring enough to invite me along."

"You don't have to thank me."

"Yes, I do. You could have just left me behind."

"No. I couldn't. I could never do that."

# -10-

Scott was on his tractor, plowing his new field, when Joyce drove into the yard.

She'd been thinking a lot lately. She was tired of working. She needed a break. And she liked this guy Scott. She liked him a lot. She thought he liked her too. Today was the day she intended to find out if there was a chance at a relationship.

She stepped out of her SUV and waved at him. He took off his straw cowboy hat and waved it back at her. Then he lifted the plow from the earth and drove the tractor over to where she stood.

"Hey, there, cowboy. Or would 'Farmer Scott' fit you better?"

"I think 'cowboy' sounds more macho. How have you been?"

"I've been fine. But I need some advice. I hope you don't mind me dropping in unannounced."

"No, not at all. It just so happens I've got something I wanted to talk to you about too. Let's go in the house and get something cold to drink."

Joyce liked the way the sweat glistened on his arms. There was something sexy about a sweaty man. Maybe because it signified hard work to her, and hard work meant success. At least she'd always equated the two together. She followed him into the house, then the kitchen.

"Why don't you sit down, Scott. You've been working harder than me. I'll fix the drinks. What'll you have?"

"I just made a pitcher of sweet tea. That sounds good. It's in the fridge. There's also some fresh squeezed lemonade in there if you want some of that."

"No, tea sounds good to me too," she said as she pressed two tall tea glasses against the ice dispenser.

Scott watched her from across the room. He liked the way her jeans hugged her hips and backside.

"Scott, you know I made a good sized commission when you bought this place."

"That's good. You worked extra hard twisting my arm to buy it, so you deserve something for your efforts."

"Oh, crap. You had your mind made up to buy it before we even met."

"True. Guilty as charged, your honor."

"I got the check a couple of days ago, and I've been wondering what to do with it. I mean, it's enough to pay off my mortgage, with enough left over to expand my kitchen and install a Jacuzzi on my back deck.

"But, if what you say is true about the power going out, I'm thinking the smart move might be to use it to prepare for the inevitable. Any thoughts?"

Scott took a sip of his tea and chose his words carefully.

"I hate being in debt to a bank or anybody else. I've always been a guy who paid cash when I could. But these are special circumstances, and yes, I am certain this thing is going to happen. I just don't know when.

"Paying off your mortgage would be a very good thing. Ordinarily I'd recommend it. But here's the thing. When the blackout happens, everybody is going to pretty much own their houses anyway. I mean, not technically. But all of their mortgage records are going to be tied up on bank computers that can never be retrieved.

"And even if they could be retrieved, it wouldn't matter. Nobody will be going to work anymore. What would they do? Walk from their homes to blacked out offices where the machines no longer worked, and just sit and look at each other? Are the banks going to evict every one of their mortgage holders?

"No, when the shit hits the fan, the whole world is going to be so focused on survival that the last thing they'll worry about is making a mortgage payment. So any money you spend paying off your mortgage will be money down the drain.

"And that brings up something I wanted to talk to you about anyway."

Her eyebrows went up. She said, "Yes?"

"I don't want to pressure you. And I don't want to mislead you. After all, there's a chance that I'm just totally crazy and this whole solar storm and EMP blackout will never happen. I'd feel terrible if I twisted your arm to do something and you came to regret it later on."

He paused for a moment and she said, "Go on…"

"Instead, I'll just tell you what I would do in your situation. I wouldn't worry about paying off my mortgage. If I'm right, property rights and deeds won't be worth the paper they're written on in a couple of years anyway. If it were me, I'd take that money and use it for something more substantial. Something that would help ensure my survival in the years ahead. Food stores. Seed stores. Equipment like generators. Materials to build Foley cages to protect essential electronics. That kind of thing."

She looked at him and said, "If I were to invest the money in all of that kind of stuff, where would I put it?"

They both knew the answer, but she ached to hear him say the words anyway.

"Here. You can make plans to come into the compound with us. I know you have no children or siblings. I never asked if your parents were still alive. But you can bring them in too."

"Are you asking me just because you need someone to help with the chores? Or is there another reason?"

Scott was afraid she was going to ask that question. He wasn't even sure he had an answer for her. But she'd backed him into a corner now. He had to answer.

"Joyce, I… I don't know what I feel, but I feel… something. I've been accused of letting my crotch do my thinking in the past, and I've probably been guilty. But this is more than a physical attraction. I don't know what it is. I don't know if it's because I feel a certain kinship to you because you can understand where I'm coming from on this whole thing. Or if something deep inside me wants to see if there's enough feeling there to make a relationship work.

"I know that's a non-answer. But this whole thing has my head spinning, and I'm very confused. And there's another factor involved too."

"Go on…"

"I've invited Linda, the boys' mother, to join us as well. I wouldn't feel right not offering her a chance to survive."

"I see. Is Linda married?"

"No. She has a boyfriend. But he's a dirt bag. I'm not sure she'd bring him along."

"Do you and Linda still have feelings for one another?"

"No. I don't know. I don't think so. I mean, we have a history, sure. But on my part I consider her just a good friend and nothing more."

"And on her part?"

"I think she would bend over backwards to make a relationship work if I offered her the chance. But I have no intention of offering her one."

Joyce put down her tea glass and said, "No. They're both dead. My parents, I mean. It's just me and my two cats. Dusty and Daisy. I used to have an old hound dog named Roy, but he was always chewing on my shoes. Every time I'd get dressed to go somewhere nice, I'd have to go looking for my shoes and hope they weren't in pieces. Roy died a year ago, bless his heart. I was going to get another puppy. But I didn't have enough shoes left to feed him. Besides, cats are much more suited to country living, I think. Plenty of mice and birds for them to chase and eat."

"Does that mean you'll join us?"

"How can I resist such a warm and heartfelt invitation?"

Scott turned red.

"I know I'm not the best at explaining myself. But I really think we'd make a good team. And there's so much to do that I don't think I can get it all done alone."

"You don't have to explain, Scott. I'm not a timid woman who will be scared off just because there's another female in the picture. And it just so happens that I'm between men right now, so I'm available to just throw caution to the wind and join you on your little project. Under one condition."

"And what is that?"

"If Linda feels threatened by me, if she doesn't want me around because she wants you all to herself, or feels intimidated by me…"

She looked him in the eyes.

"If that happens, you have to promise not to give in to her and try to kick me out of here. If I commit to this, and put my own money into it, then it'll be my home as well as yours. I will not have you show me the door based on the whims of an insecure woman."

"You have my word. And you don't know me enough to know this. Not yet. But someday you'll understand that my word is my bond. I've never broken a promise in my life. And I have no intention of starting."

Joyce smiled.

"Okay, then, cowboy, I just have one more question."

"Yes?"

"When I pulled in I saw about a hundred uprooted trees laying on their sides and lined up in a pretty row a quarter mile long. What's that all about?"

He laughed and said, "Come on. Let's take a walk around *our* new home. I'll show you what I've been up to for the last few weeks."

# -11-

Joyce continued to work two days a week, just to keep her hands in the pot in case Scott's theory was all fantasy. But most of her days were spent preparing for the end of civilization as she knew it.

Scott was right. There were a thousand and one things that needed to be done. Much too much for one person to handle.

She settled into a routine. Each morning she didn't go to the office, she'd arise about six, shower and have breakfast, and feed her cats. Then she'd make a trip to her local Walmart to shop.

Joyce didn't shop the way most people do, though. She took the rear seats out of her Honda CRV and left them in her garage. When she pulled into the Walmart parking lot she had the intention of filling every square inch.

Her first few visits were hit and miss until she developed a system. Then she got it down to a science.

The first two trips in and out of the store were for canned goods. She'd determined that two full carts of canned goods did a pretty good job of covering the floor space of her vehicle.

Then she went back inside for two more carts full of other foods that had a very long shelf life. Dry beans and pasta, rice and spaghetti, Ramen noodles. Some canned goods, like Vienna sausages and canned ham, had shelf lives of four years. So did the canned spaghetti sauce, and it was high in calories, which was another plus. She also stocked up on sugar and flour and baking goods, and dry milk and seasonings.

These goods went on top of the canned goods. If there was still space, she went back in for more supplies. Bags of charcoal, pillows and blankets, coats and linens. And whatever else she thought they'd need for the long term.

She was always cautious not to buy anything which had to be refrigerated. That would come later. The first project on her list of things to do was to build a food supply at the compound, that would get them through their first few months if the EMPs hit in the fall. They reasoned that if the power went out in the late summer or fall, it would be April before they could plant subsistence crops. And late the following summer before they could be harvested. The Walmart food was to keep them alive in the interim.

And if they had time to grow their crops and put them aside before the power went out? Well, that was okay too. As Joyce told Scott, having too much food was much better than not having enough. If they didn't need the Walmart food initially, they could eat it later on before it expired, canning their home grown crops for later use.

After two months shopping at Walmart, Joyce had filled up one of the extra bedrooms with canned and dry foods, sorted and marked with their expiration dates. They were arranged so that the items expiring first were located on the top and front of each stack. That would ensure nothing spoiled before it was eaten.

Once the dry stock was assembled, Joyce went on to her second project. She'd helped her grandmother and then her mother can fruits and vegetables when she was a little girl growing up in Lubbock. She remembered it as being fun.

She found out that from an adult's perspective, especially when canning on a large scale, it was actually a lot of work.

But she still enjoyed it.

And she learned that she could can not just fruits and vegetables, but also cooked meats and boiled eggs as well. So for an additional three months, she continued her frequent visits to Walmart. Only this time the back of her SUV held eight large coolers. She filled some of them with whole chickens, prime ribs, beef and pork roasts, and various sausages. Others were filled with a wide variety of fresh produce.

She went to Walmart twice a week now, and two days a week she spent at the compound, baking and canning her haul from the previous day. After three months she had literally hundreds of quart jars of anything and everything. When the space she'd set aside in the basement was finally full, she said she'd finally had enough and vowed never to can anything again.

Of course she knew better. If Scott was right about the solar storms and the EMPs, she'd spend the rest of her life in the compound. During the warm weather months they'd be growing and harvesting crops. And she'd be canning a good portion of the crops for the winter months. But for now she was just tired of it.

Her third project wasn't quite as much work. She visited Walmart again, to buy two hundred one pound blocks of cheese. Not all from one store, of course. She was considerate of others and only took about half of what each store had on the shelves. Then she'd move down the road to the next Walmart and do the same thing. She didn't think it proper, after all, to inconvenience other shoppers who might also need cheese.

After she got all her cheese and packed it in a side by side refrigerator at the compound, she spent four days melting red cheese wax in a pot on the stove. Once melted, she dipped each block of cheese in the wax, wrapped it in cheesecloth and then put it aside on waxed paper to cool and dry.

She put four coats of wax on each block of cheese and then wrapped each in waxed paper. Then she lined them up on top of boxes of supplies that were in the basement storage room. The cheese would keep unrefrigerated for many years.

In her prepper days Joyce had learned that eggs will keep unrefrigerated for up to a year if they're coated in mineral oil. Scott had planned to purchase chickens and roosters and to build a chicken coop in the back of the compound. He didn't bother to tell Joyce, though, until after she'd purchased fifty dozen eggs, treated them and stacked them neatly in the same back bedroom as the dry goods.

"I'm sorry, Sugar," Scott said. "I should have told you before you went through all that trouble."

She countered, "Oh, it's no problem. I hope you like eggs, because that's what you're getting for breakfast every morning for the next year."

Scott did indeed like eggs. And the thought of Joyce waking up next to him every morning for a year appealed to him. They were becoming closer and closer with each passing day. Being heavily involved on their mission helped. It also helped that they found they had the same interests and hobbies.

Scott asked, "So, now what are you going to work on, since you've got our food stores all set?"

"It's funny you should ask. I want you to teach me how to drive that tractor, so I can help you with some of the outside chores. I'm tired of being cooped up inside all day while you're out in the sunshine."

"You really want to learn?"

"Yep. And I want to drive that little Bobcat of yours too. It looks like a lot of fun."

Scott had plowed under the field north of the compound where he planned to plant crops in the spring. But he found the soil was a lot rockier than he'd thought.

The pair walked out to look it over.

"I hooked up the rake attachment that came in yesterday. It works just like a hard garden rake. We'll drag it across the plowed land and it'll drag the rocks to the end of each row. A lot of them will slip through the forks of the rake, though, so we'll have to do it several times. Once we get them all gathered at the end of the rows, we'll use the bucket on the Bobcat to pick them up and move them out of here."

"Well, that's not hard. It shouldn't take more than a couple of days."

"Don't kid yourself. That's just the first step. Many of the rocks are still buried. After we're done, we'll replow the field. More of the rocks will come to the surface. And then we'll go through the same process again.

"We'll probably have to go through the process four times, maybe five, to get all the rocks out of the soil. But that's not even half the task."

"Oh, yeah? Why not?"

"Because that'll only clear the first ten inches of soil. It'll be fine for wheat and sorghum, but corn has a deeper root system."

"Okay. So how do we work around that?"

"We'll use the bucket on the Bobcat to dig out the first ten inches of clean soil. Basically, we'll dig a ten inch hole in the ground an acre and a half wide. Then we'll plow the next ten inches and repeat the process all over again. It'll be tedious and time consuming, but in the end we'll have twice the crop yield."

Joyce was impressed.

"How did you find out so much about farming?"

He laughed.

"The internet."

"Okay, Mister Farmer, you mentioned wheat, sorghum and corn. Why those three crops?"

"Three different crops, so that we can alternate the types of nutrients we pull from the ground each year. Farmers who plant the same crop in the same ground year after year eventually see a dramatic drop in their yield. They simply pull the nutrients from the soil faster than Mother Nature can replace them.

"Different crops pull different types of nutrients from the soil. So the first year, we'll plant a corn crop. We'll grow as much as we can, and then we'll store it in 55 gallon drums. We'll grow sweet corn. It'll be good enough for us to eat as corn, or we can make corn meal from it. Or corn bread or tortillas, or breading for meats. We can use it a hundred different ways. It will also yield several gallons of corn oil for cooking. And as a pinch, it can be used as cattle feed. And the pigs will love the cobs. It's like candy to them.

"The second year we'll grow sorghum. Cattle feed. By the second year, our initial stock of hay bales will be pretty much gone. So we'll try to grow enough sorghum for three to four years. We'll bag it into fifty pound sacks and stack it in one of the barns. And we'll use it for winter feed, when the snow is too thick and the grass too sparse for the cattle to graze.

"The third year we'll grow wheat. And again, we'll grow as much as we can in the hopes that we can stretch it for three years until we plant another wheat crop.

"The fourth year we swing back to corn again."

"What happens if we don't grow enough of something and run out?"

"Then we learn a valuable lesson. It won't be the end of the world. I mean, if we run low on something, we'll make modifications. During the off-season, between harvest and planting, we can expand our growing field. Make it larger. Or we can plant it earlier in the season and see if we can grow a second crop before cold weather sets in.

"In other words, we do what farmers have been doing for thousands of years. We adjust."

# -12-

Scott left the compound early enough to beat the boys home from school. Zachary's bus was running late, as usual, and Jordan beat him home.

"Hi, Dad."

"Hi, pal. How was school?"

"It sucks. As usual. I can't wait to graduate. My life will be sooooo much easier."

Scott couldn't help but chuckle. If his son only knew.

"You understand, don't you, son, that high school is the fun time in your life? When you get out, you either go to college, where the work is much harder. Or you go to work where you have a boss who rides your ass all day long.

"And whichever way you go, you have bills to pay, checkbooks to balance, responsibilities to others."

"Great! Thanks for reminding me that after high school my life is over. What would I do without you, Dad?"

"Don't forget that when your mom and I get old it's going to be your responsibility to take care of us."

Jordan's jaw dropped.

"You never told me that before."

"Sure. When we get too old to take care of ourselves, you'll have to do it for us. You can't just abandon us on somebody's doorstep, you know. You'll have to feed us with a spoon when our teeth fall out and we can't move so much anymore. Change our diapers…"

Jordan interrupted him.

"I soooo don't want to hear this."

Scott laughed. Jordan looked at him, not knowing whether he was kidding. So he did what teenagers were good at. He deflected the conversation by changing the subject.

"What's for dinner, Dad? I don't smell anything cooking."

"We're going to Perico's. Best Mexican food in San Antonio. I didn't feel like cooking."

"All right!" Jordan pumped his fist. "Best news I've heard all day."

At that precise moment the phone rang. Jordan looked at the caller ID. It was Linda.

"Hi Mom. How are you?"

"I'm fine, baby. I just wanted to tell your dad not to make dinner. I've got lasagna in the oven. He hasn't started cooking yet, has he?"

"Uh, no, Mom." Technically, it was the truth. But he was crestfallen. He'd have to wait til another day to savor Perico's beef and potato empanadas.

"Good. Is he around? Can I talk to him?"

"Sure, Mom. Here he is."

"Hello, Linda. How are you?"

"I'm well, Scott. I'm glad I caught you before you started cooking. Are you still going to drop the boys off at six?"

"Uh, yes. We're just waiting for Zach's bus to come, and then we'll pack their bags and head out. We were going to stop for dinner, but we'll do that another time. Is that why you mentioned my cooking? Do you already have plans?"

"Yes. I've got lasagna in the oven. I hope that's okay."

"Sure, it's no problem at all. We can eat out anytime and they love your lasagna."

"Scott, there was something else I wanted to ask you as well."

"Okay. Shoot."

"I feel guilty that you're going through all that work to get your compound ready up there, and I want to help in some way. Is there anything I can do to make it easier on you?"

He thought for a moment.

"Well, we still have a lot of computer work to be done."

"What kind of computer work? Like research?"

"Yes, exactly. I've been making a list of research materials that might come in handy after the power grids go down. We'll have computers that we'll protect from the EMPs. But the internet will be down. It won't come back up for years if at all. So we won't just be able to jump on line when we have a question."

"Okay. Just tell me what to do."

"I'll give you my list when I drop off the boys. It has things on it like how to do first aid. How to stock a new lake to keep the fish from dying. How to get rid of rats and ticks. How to birth a pig stuck in the birth canal. All kinds of strange things that might come in handy.

"What I'd like for you to do is just search for as much information on the subjects. Take snapshots of each page and save each snapshot as a .jpg file. For the text, copy and paste it to a Word document.

"Then, after you're done, I'll bring you half a dozen toner cartridges and a couple of reams of paper. You can start printing everything out. You may have ten thousand pages or more by the time you're done. And much of it may never be used. But if we do need some information later, and have no other way to get it, then it'll come in real handy."

Linda said, "Okay. Good. I have a couple of free hours most evenings, I'll start working the list tonight, while the boys are playing their video games."

"Atta girl, and thanks for your help."

"Hey, it's no problem. Thanks for letting me get involved."

"No sweat. Did you put that bike in your trunk like I asked?"

"Yes. Along with the backpack."

"Did Glen give you a hard time about it?"

"A little. He asked why I had it and I told him I might decide to go for a ride occasionally."

"And what did he say?"

"He mumbled something about my fat ass and him not holding his breath."

"That's Glen, all right. Mister Charming."

"I know. Anyway, I have to go check on the lasagna and fix some salads. I'll see you in a bit."

"Okay. Bye now."

Scott hung up the phone just in time to hear Zach slam the front door.

"Hey, Booger! How was your day?"

"Fine, Dad. School was a drag, though. Thank God it's Friday."

"Yes, indeed. Go upstairs and pack your bag for your mom's house. She's got dinner waiting for you."

He watched his youngest son bounding up the stairs. He hoped he was wrong about the solar storms. He couldn't bear to think of his boys suffering in any way. They'd been the one constant in his life for a long time. And the one thing that kept him going on his worst days.

# -13-

Spring turned into summer and the days grew hot. Even at the compound outside of Junction, where the elevation was several hundred feet higher than in San Antonio, it was painfully hot.

Joyce was glad to be working in the Bobcat now. It had an enclosed cab, complete with a small air conditioner. The tractor was open air. It subjected the driver not only to the unrelenting rays of the sun, but also to whatever dust and dirt the tractor kicked up.

The Bobcat was much more comfortable. And it was fun too. Like driving an oversized Tonka toy.

They'd finished raking out the rocks, and had dumped them in a huge pile at the end of the field. Now Joyce spent her days scooping up the clean dirt they'd made in the bucket of the Bobcat and moving it out of the way. After they'd cleared off the first ten inches of rock-free soil, they'd plow the area again. And they'd repeat the process. When the second ten inches of soil was free of rocks, they'd put the first layer back. And they'd have twenty inches of clean soil to farm with.

She saw Scott driving up on his Gator and put the Bobcat in neutral. She slid open the driver's window and said, "Hey, cowboy! What are you up to?"

"Hey, babe. Are you coming out here tomorrow?"

"No, I've got three properties to show tomorrow. You'll have to get by without me. Why?"

"I just need to borrow the Bobcat for a couple of days."

"To do what?"

"I need to put the auger attachment on it and drill some fence post holes. I just got a call from a friend who works at one of the cement companies. They're breaking ground on four new housing developments west of town next month. He says cement and concrete are going to be hard to get and are going to shoot up in price for awhile. He said if I had any projects going on to schedule the trucks now."

"Does he know about this place and what we're doing here?"

"No. He was the broker when I expanded a couple of my storage places. He's always looking for a commission, so he's in the habit of calling me occasionally to see if I need any work done."

"What did you tell him?"

"I told him I had a good friend who was building a church summer camp in the mountains near Kerrville. And that I thought they were going to need some concrete work done. I said I'd be his go-between and broker the deal, in exchange for a couple of beers."

Joyce laughed.

"So he won't figure it out when he gets the check and it's got your signature on it?"

"Nope. Because I'm going to transfer the money into your account, and you're going to write the check."

"Oh, so I'm the friend who's building the church camp. Sneaky… I like the way you think."

Joyce went back to digging her pit, and Scott went to the west side of the house. The day before he'd bought a one thousand yard spool of twine and fifty wooden stakes. He hammered one of the wooden stakes at the front corner of the house and tied the end of the twine onto it. Then he paced off fifty yards, unwinding the twine as he went.

Fifty yards from the house, he hammered in another stake, pulled the twine tight, and wrapped it around the stake several times. Then he went an additional fifty yards.

He was now one hundred yards away from the house. Here he placed another stake, wrapped the twine around it, and turned ninety degrees to the north.

When Scott finished an hour later, he had staked out a fence line that extended one hundred yards on each side of the house, and north from the front edge of the house for one hundred yards. When the fence was installed, only the front face of the house would be visible from the driveway. The front face of the house and a ten foot high steel privacy fence.

But he wasn't finished yet. Inside the massive compound, at exactly the halfway point, he ran another fence line. This one would be a standard wooden privacy fence, six feet tall, to split the compound in half. It would separate the livestock pens and chicken coop from the front half of the compound, mainly as a means of providing a comfortable living area that didn't smell like a stockyard.

It would also provide growing space for a quarter acre garden that would be free of wandering cattle, pigs and chickens.

It was in this front half of the compound that Scott staked out places for four concrete pads. Each pad was about the size of a two car garage. The first three pads would be the new homes of Butler buildings, which were prefabricated barnlike structures that could be delivered and installed in a single afternoon.

In one barn Scott would fabricate a huge Foley cage, which would protect everything inside it. Once done, he'd fill it full of vehicles, equipment, electronic items, and luxury items, such as televisions and microwaves and such. Basically everything a normal house could plug into the wall or drive to and from someplace else.

Another barn would hold food stores, like bulk corn stored in 55 gallon drums or rice and flour in fifty pound sacks. It would double as Scott's tool shed.

The third barn would hold feed for the livestock. Hay for the horses and field corn for the pigs, initially. Later, when they started growing their own feed, it would hold wheat or sorghum.

The fourth pad was unique. The size and shape of a two car garage, only the outside three feet of the floor would be concrete. The interior of the floor would be bare ground, and once poured it would resemble a bizarre type of square donut.

It was on this pad that Scott would build his greenhouse.

Scott had decided early on that he wanted to provide his family members with a wide variety of fruits and vegetables after they were sealed off from the rest of the world.

Some fruits and vegetables would grow very well in the higher altitude and cooler air of the Kerrville mountains. He planned an orchard of apple, peach and pecan trees northwest of the compound, near the fishing pond.

However, there were some things that required warmer temperatures.

That's where the greenhouse came in. Once the donut hole was poured, Scott's plans were to use an excavator to dig out four feet or so of earth from the center of the hole. He'd truck in enough prime topsoil to replace it, and then build a greenhouse around it.

Once the greenhouse was built, he'd be able to grow citrus inside the building, even when there was snow on the ground in the wintertime.

He'd planned to plant orange, lemon and avocado trees in the center of the greenhouse. Along the outside perimeter he'd have a series of planter boxes where he could grow grapes and various types of berries in the winter months. They might be isolated from the rest of the world, but they'd still eat fairly well.

Scott went to his workroom and retrieved a hundred foot cloth tape on a large reel, with a hand crank on the side. He took it back to where he'd started this project several hours before. To the first wooden stake he'd hammered into the ground at the southwest corner of the house.

He tacked the end of the tape measure to the front of the stake and reeled it out along the twine he'd laid out earlier. And every ten feet, all the way around the fence line, he sprayed an "x" on the ground in fluorescent orange spray paint.

By the time he finished, the sun was sinking low in the western sky. His back was breaking, and his feet hurt.

But he felt good. He felt he'd accomplished more on this one day than he had in a long time. And when he stepped back twenty yards and used his imagination, he could finally envision what his compound would eventually look like.

He sat in his pickup truck and cranked the engine. With the cool air washing over his sweaty face and Taylor Swift serenading him softly in the background, he picked up his cell phone and called his friend at Alamo Cement.

"Hey, Rob, how are you doing?"

"Very good, Scott. You got any projects going on?"

"Not me, personally, no. But that friend I told you about does. The one who's building some kind of church summer camp up around Kerrville. She's ready for some portable building slabs and a boatload of fence post anchors, if she can get it for a good price."

"How much we talking?"

"About seventy yards."

"Okay. That'll be worth the trip. Let me crunch some numbers and I'll get back with you tomorrow, okay?"

"Sounds good. Talk to you then."

Scott hung up his phone, cranked up his CD, and sang "Fifteen" along with Taylor Swift as he pulled out of the drive and headed back to San Antonio.

She didn't need his help.

# -14-

As summer stretched into fall, everything seemed to be slowly falling into place. Then Scott had a nightmare one night at the end of September. He dreamed that the blackout happened, and he was nowhere near ready. He hadn't even built his Foley cages yet, and all his vehicles and equipment were ruined. The blackout happened in the middle of the night, none of his vehicles would work, and he, Linda and the boys had to hike seventy miles over the course of two weeks to get to the unfinished compound. Their mom bitched and moaned every step of the way.

Scott had woken up that night in a cold sweat.

But looking back, his nightmare had actually been a good thing. It reminded him that he didn't know when the EMPs were coming. And that he needed to do a better job of prioritizing his tasks, so that the most important things got done first. That would minimize the problems if he was caught off guard.

After his fence posts were set and the slabs poured for his outbuildings, he had the Butler buildings delivered. It took him a solid week of screwing sheet metal to the interior walls, ceiling and floor of one building, followed by a layer of thick plywood. But when he was finished, it was a secure place that was large enough to hold a lot of equipment.

Inside the Foley Barn he placed a brand new Ford pickup that he leased for one of his rental units, two leased Gators, another used tractor he'd picked up on the internet, and a wide array of household appliances and electronics. Also included were a wide assortment of vehicle parts and batteries. Not only would these vehicles survive the blackout, but he'd be able to keep them running for decades.

He also built a similar Foley Barn in his back yard in north San Antonio, but on a smaller scale. This one was built inside an oversized tool shed. It was just big enough to hold two all wheel drive Gators, a case of flashlight batteries and several pairs of night vision goggles. If the blackout happened while they were in San Antonio, these would be their escape vehicles.

Another thing the nightmare pointed out to him was that he was moving at a snail's pace. Every time he finished a project, two more cropped up to replace it. He and Joyce had been trying to do most of the construction work themselves, and they were wearing themselves too thin.

Scott Harter was a hard headed man. But he was also a realist. And he realized that as much as he'd like to do everything himself, or with Joyce's help, it just couldn't be done.

So the day after his nightmare, he contracted out for two things: the installation of a ham radio antenna, and a builder to install his greenhouse for him. His logic was that if the blackout occurred next month, everything else could be done after they assembled in the compound. That wouldn't be the most ideal of circumstances, but it would be acceptable.

The greenhouse and the radio antenna, on the other hand, were essential. The greenhouse would help ensure their comfort in the years ahead. The antenna would help ensure their security.

Joyce finished clearing out the pit, and plowed up the deeper layer of dirt. Then she began raking the rocks out of it, just as Scott had showed her. She was quite an asset, and he knew it. He told her constantly how important she was to him. Her response was always the same: "I know it, cowboy. And you'd better not forget it."

Scott went back to building his fence. The posts had been placed before the concrete was poured, and now stood as a long line of lonely sentinels around the property. He used a portable welding rig that he dragged around with a Gator as he went from post to post to post and welded one inch square boxed steel, three pieces to each post.

It was a long process. He figured it would take two months of long workdays just to get the crosspieces on. And he was already tired of the grind.

He'd never win any awards for his welding talents. His beads were rough and sloppy. But they were strong, and that's what counted.

The panels had already been delivered and were stacked in twenty piles on the ground just outside the fence line. They weren't made for fences. They were panels for steel roofing. But they were perfect for Scott's needs. Ten feet long and corrugated, they would fit together easily. They were guaranteed by the manufacturer not to rust for thirty years. Not that that mattered much to Scott. The manufacturer's guarantee wouldn't amount to a hill of beans once the power went out around the world and the manufacturer was out of business.

But Scott's logic was sound. If these panels would last for thirty years lying flat, with occasional standing water from rainstorms, then they'd likely last several times that standing up.

He was about a month into his fence project when Jordan came to him and asked if he could get a job.

"Why?"

"Oh, you know, Dad. A guy needs money for taking his girl out and stuff. You weren't always so old. You remember. Or did they have girls when you were a kid?"

Zachary chimed in from the couch, "Oh, they had girls. They just didn't have cars back then, so Dad had to ride his brontosaurus when he took a girl out."

Scott enjoyed the harassment his sons gave him. He'd been a smartass all his life, and the apples hadn't fallen far from the tree.

"What kind of job are you talking about?"

"I don't know. Flipping burgers probably. Or making tacos at the Burrito Hut. There aren't a lot of jobs for high school kids."

"What kind of money do those jobs pay?"

"Crappy money. Minimum wage. seven bucks an hour. But like I said, that's all there is."

"Maybe not. There are jobs out there that pay a lot better than that, if you're willing to work hard."

"You know I work hard, Dad. Shoot, I do all the yard work without even being asked. And you know I've always helped you out clearing out those storage lockers when people abandoned them. What kind of jobs are you talking about?"

"Working for me. For pay this time. Not just because you're a good son."

Jordan raised a wary eyebrow.

"Doing what, exactly?"

"I need help building a fence up at the compound. It's not difficult. But it's very labor intensive, and very monotonous. Just putting metal panels up, drilling holes through them, and then screwing them into place."

Jordan saw that his Dad was serious. It was negotiation time.

"That sounds like a thirty dollar an hour job. With benefits."

Scott laughed.

"I'll tell you what. I'll pay you twenty. And I'll give you a ride to and from work every Saturday and Sunday."

"Are you serious? Twenty bucks an hour? Deal!"

Zachary had been listening in from his vantage point on the couch.

"Hey, how come he gets all the good stuff and I never do?"

"I'll tell you what, Zach. He's gonna need a helper. If you're willing to help him, I'll pay you fifteen dollars an hour."

"How come he gets twenty and I only get fifteen?"

"Bosses always get paid more than workers."

"He'll be my boss?"

"Yep. But being a boss isn't always so fun. Whenever y'all screw up, I won't yell at you. I'll yell at him instead. And you can watch."

"Deal."

And so it was that Scott found two willing laborers to help him finish that damned fence, which had been becoming a thorn in his side.

"Wait a minute, Dad. What about Mom? We normally go over there on the weekends."

"I'll talk to your mom about it. She's been saying that she misses cooking for you guys and helping you with your homework. I'll make a deal with her. Jordan, you can drive your car over there every afternoon instead of coming home. You can do your homework and have dinner there.

"Zach, I'll go by your school tomorrow and change your bus arrangements. You can take a different bus to your mom's house."

"Do you think Mom will be okay with it?"

"Sure she will. She knows she can come up to the compound any time on the weekends to help if she wants to. So she can still hang with you on the weekends if she wants. But she'll get more weekday time with you now. And it'll help me out because I can work up there longer during the week without having to come home to cook for you guys. I can stay a couple extra hours and pick you up at your mom's around ten or so.

"I don't know why I didn't think of this sooner."

# -15-

The following Saturday morning, Scott and the boys pulled into the compound. It was the boys' first time there, and they were in awe.

"Wow, Dad. It's huge!"

"Yeah, it's pretty good size. It'll have to be, to have everything we need to survive."

"How long do you think we'll have to stay up here?"

"I don't know, son. At least until the world is civilized and safe again. And maybe they find a way to get the power grids up and running again, and start repairing the vehicles and electronics. I doubt if it'll happen before you're old and gray."

Zachary said, "But Dad, if we're up here, how are we ever gonna meet chicks?"

It was something Scott had never thought of. He'd just assumed that the boys would raise families of their own, and they would continue life in the compound after Scott had passed on. Zach's question was a valid one, and one for which he had no answer.

"I don't know, Zach. Maybe after we get settled in and the world adjusts to the changes, we can venture out and meet some of the neighbors. Maybe they'll have some hot chicks who are just itching to meet some good lookin' dudes."

Jordan commented dryly, "First of all, Dad, I don't think anyone has used the word 'dudes' since the seventies. And second, I'd settle for even an average chick. I'm a teenage boy, remember? With the raging hormones and all that stuff?"

"Where did you hear about raging hormones?"

"In sex education."

"Did they teach you about abstinence?"

"Sure, but I never thought I'd actually have to do it."

Zachary asked, "What's abstinence?"

"That's when you don't have a girlfriend."

"Oh. Like now."

"Exactly."

Joyce stepped out of the Bobcat and walked over to the truck as the guys were getting out of it.

"So these are the boys I've heard so much about."

Scott introduced them.

"This is Jordan, my oldest. And Zachary, my youngest. Boys, this is Joyce."

They shook hands, and Jordan said, "Dad told us you're going to be living up here with us. Do you have any teenaged daughters?"

Joyce laughed a bit nervously and said, "No, I'm afraid not. Why?"

"Oh, nothing. Just wondering."

Scott looked at Joyce and asked, "You tired of raking rocks yet?"

"You're behind the times, cowboy. I finished raking all the rocks two days ago. Now I'm putting all the soil back in the pit. I should be done with that in three or four days."

"Wow, I'm impressed. I always did love fast women."

Everyone except Scott and Zachary rolled their eyes. Scott because he thought he was being clever, and Zach because he didn't understand the term.

"So you'll be ready for another project in three or four days?"

"Nope. I didn't say that. I said I'd be finished with this one in three or four days. Then I'm taking a few days off before I start something else. I've earned it from getting saddle sores from that damn tractor."

Scott couldn't argue. She'd been working awfully hard, after all.

"Tell you what. How about next weekend we drive on up to Fredericksburg for some good German food? To celebrate the completion of the field project and the new blisters on the boys' hands?"

Jordan and Zach looked at each other.

"Dad, we don't have any blisters on our hands."

Scott chuckled.

"Not yet, son. Not yet."

Jordan didn't like the sound of that. But he was going to be paid almost three times what his friends were getting at the burger joint. And he wasn't afraid of hard work. Never had been. So he was okay with a few blisters.

Zachary was a trooper. He was okay too.

"Come on, boys. Let's get you started."

He took them to the tool barn and gave them each a pair of gloves and a tool apron. Each apron had two large pockets in front, and a loop on each side to hold tools.

He took a large box of sheet metal screws and poured a good amount into three of the four pockets. In the fourth, he put a half dozen quarter inch drill bits.

"These are hardened steel tipped bits," he said. They're made for cutting through steel. But even with these kind of bits, you'll go through a lot of them. You'll be drilling hundreds of holes, and you'll just flat wear them out. Hell, you'll probably burn up three or four drills too, before we're finished."

He took two cordless drills and three spare batteries and said, "Jordan, grab that ladder and follow me."

Scott led the boys to the corner of the house where he'd started the project weeks before. He took the first panel of corrugated metal roofing from one of the stacks and held it up against the three crosspieces.

"Okay, guys. The concept is a simple one. But even though it doesn't require a lot of thinking, it requires that you both pay attention. It's easy to get hurt if you're not careful. The edges of these things are sharp and can slice your arm or face right open if you're not careful. Always wear your gloves when you're handing it, and always watch what you're doing.

"Zachary, take those ear buds out of your ears. You can listen to your music when you're not working. While you're here working with your brother, the two of you need to be able to communicate. You can't do that with ear buds in your ears.

"Okay, I'm going to position the first piece, and then I want you to hold it into place while I drill the holes and place the screws.

After placing the panel perpendicular to the house and flush up against it, the boys held it firmly in place. Scott used one drill to drill three holes through the center of the panel and into the center crosspiece behind it. Then he placed the drill on the ground and picked up the second drill. The second drill had a bit driver in it that fit the sheet metal screws in the boys' aprons. He pulled three screws from Jordan's apron pocket and used the drill to drive the screws into the holes he'd just drilled.

"Okay, you can let go now."

The boys let go of the piece of metal and took a couple of steps back.

"The first three screws will hold it into place while you do the rest of the drilling. Once you're at this point, you drill three similar holes in the bottom, through the roofing and into the crosspiece behind it. You do three holes on the top crosspiece too. Then you use the other drill to install the screws. Any questions?"

Zachary said, "Nope. Piece of cake."

Jordan said, "When do we get to take a coffee break?"

Scott said, "You're fired. Zach, you're the boss now."

"All right! Hey, wait a minute. You're kidding, right?"

Scott laughed.

"Yeah, but just barely."

He went on with his instruction.

"These things are corrugated and I chose this design for a reason. Once the first piece is placed, the rest will be easy. You don't have to worry about the pieces going up crooked or off center. All you do is overlap the first channel of the new piece into the last channel of the piece you just put up. They'll fit together perfectly. As long as you do that, the fence will be perfectly square. And it'll be strong, too. In addition to the nine screws holding each panel into place, the panel on each side of it will also hold it up. This fence will outlive you, boys, mark my words. But we have to do it right. No skipped screws. No holes drilled through the panel that miss the crosspiece behind it. Understood?"

Both boys shook their heads yes.

"One last thing. Have either of you ever used a cordless drill before?"

Jordan looked at his brother and then answered for both of them.

"No sir."

"Okay, the first thing you'll notice is that they're heavy. Very heavy. You don't have to hassle with a cord, but the tradeoff is that the batteries are heavier than the drill. After a few hours at this your arms will feel like they're going to fall off. There are two of you, so you can trade off the drilling and the panel holding. You can take breaks to let your arms rest when you need to. I won't say anything unless I notice you're breaking more than you're working. Understand?"

"Yes sir."

"Now, then, if the cordless drills kick your ass and you just can't lift your arms to do the work anymore, then just go back to the tool barn. There are a couple of corded drills and some long extension cords in there, and you can switch out the cordless drills if you want to. The cords are a pain in the butt, but the drills only weigh half as much. So I'll leave that choice up to you. Any questions?"

"No sir."

Scott left them and went to the opposite side of the compound, where he'd left off welding the crosspieces. He knew they'd do a good job. They were his boys, after all. He'd taught them years before that anything worth doing was worth doing right.

# -16-

A few weeks later things were progressing well. Joyce took a week off from the compound, caught up on things at work and in her personal life, and came back refreshed and ready to go.

Scott finished welding the crosspieces and was spending his days building a two-hundred yard long wooden privacy fence that effectively split the compound right down the middle. Joyce worked with him on it, and they found that they worked as well together on a single project as when they were each doing their own thing.

The greenhouse was completed, and the citrus trees were planted inside them. The Butler buildings were also in, but needed to be filled with feed and hay.

Scott asked Joyce, as she was hammering a fence picket up with galvanized nails, "Hey, do you mind if I leave you alone on this project for three or four days?"

"No, cowboy. Why? What are you going to be doing?"

"I want to lease a flatbed trailer, and start buying feed and hay for the barns. Then I want to start buying the livestock."

"Are we far enough along for the livestock?"

"Yes, I think so. Most of the barbed wire is up, and if they manage to find a hole and slip out, they won't go far because of all the mesquite trees we've laid down along the perimeter. I'm afraid to wait too long. If the blackout were to hit today and we had no livestock, we'd be forced to become vegetarians for the rest of our lives."

Joyce laughed.

"Yuck! Not me, cowboy. Salads are okay, but only if you eat real food along with them."

"Yeah. My thinking exactly."

He swatted her on the bottom. She said, "You keep that up and we're going to be finished fencing for the day. You'll be nailing me instead."

Now it was his turn to laugh.

"Now, as tempted as I am, we don't need to be burning our daylight doing any of that kind of stuff. That's what night time is for."

"Party pooper."

She stuck out her lower lip and pretended to pout.

"No, if you need to stack feed in the barns and get some stock in here, go right ahead. I can finish up these pickets without you. I'll need help hanging the gate, because it's a two person job. But I'll grab the boys to help me if you're not around."

"Great. I'll start hauling feed tomorrow, then."

"And, hey, speaking of those boys, I've been impressed at how hard they're working. Do you tell them often what great boys they are? And how much you love them?"

"Yeah, sometimes. But they know."

"It doesn't matter if they know or not, bonehead. When you love somebody, you need to tell them sometimes. Words like that are food for the soul. They need to hear it, whether they know it or not."

If she was fishing, Scott didn't take the bait. Sometimes it was hard to read her. He'd suspected that she was falling for him. Or maybe already had. As for returning the feelings, he wasn't quite sure what he felt. Not yet.

Scott had been hurt several times before when it came to love. It wasn't just the whole thing with Linda. There had been a couple of women that came after Linda who broke his heart as well. And had come close to breaking his spirit.

The result was that he was no longer a man who fell in love easily.

He did know, though, that he enjoyed being with this woman. They clicked in every way possible. Was that the same as love? He wasn't sure. But he damn well wasn't going to walk into love and get hurt again. Not when there was no hurry to do so.

He looked into her eyes. He wondered if she needed the confirmation. Maybe it wasn't the boys who needed to hear those three little words. Maybe it was her.

But if she was hoping to hear him say he loved her, she seemed to take it well when he didn't. She smiled and went back to her work, and didn't seem hurt or upset in any way.

Maybe he would tell her he loved her someday soon. But first he had to fight an internal battle, a debate within his own mind, that it was love he really felt. And whether or not it was smart to risk another broken heart by falling in love again.

# -17-

"Howdy, partner."

A burley mountain of a man in a blue plaid shirt and coveralls met Scott halfway across the feed store floor.

He reached out a ham-sized fist and Scott took it. It was a firm handshake.

Scott's father had always told him you can tell a lot from a handshake. Men who shook hands with a firm grip were confident. That confidence usually came from the knowledge that they were honest and successful. They were good men to do business with.

Men with weak handshakes, on the other hand, were usually the nervous sort. Scott's father maintained that they were nervous because they had things to hide. They couldn't be trusted.

And after all his years in business, Scott had seen for himself that in nearly all cases, his father was right.

This man, who looked like he stepped right out of an old western movie, was an honest man. Scott was sure of it.

"I'm Tom Haskins. What can I do for you today, sir?"

"Scott Harter. I just bought a few acres of land, and I thought I'd fulfill a boyhood dream of mine and start my own cattle ranch. Not a big one. Just a few head. Trouble is, I don't know beans about cows or ranching. I'll learn as I go, but I was hoping you could help me figure out what kind of feed to buy."

"You're gonna be a cowboy, huh? Good for you, partner. The cowboy is a dying breed. Nobody wants to work with livestock anymore. We can use a few more good cowboys in the business.

"Come on back here and I'll give you crash course on cattle feed.

"This here's what we call compound feed. This is made by Purina, one of the best brands, but there are several other good brands also. It comes in pellet form, it's easy to scoop and measure, and economical. Cows are like teenage boys. They'll eat whatever you put in front of them. You can give them two pounds a day of this stuff, and they'll be fine. Or, you can give them ten pounds a day and they'll get fat. This is good sustenance food, for winter and droughts and such.

"This over here is called forage. It comes in bundles and is all organic material. That means anything that comes out of the ground could be caught up in here... grass, weeds, leaves, whatever. It's a lot cheaper than feed, but it takes a lot more to keep your cattle full. Plus, forage doesn't have the vitamins and supplements your cows need, so if you give them a strictly forage diet you'll have to give them vitamins to keep them healthy.

"A little more expensive than the forage, but cheaper than the compound feed, is hay bales. Hay comes in several varieties. If you have horses too, they can eat the hay also. But they can't eat the compound feed, because it's not made specifically for horses. It'll clog their intestines."

Scott was thoroughly confused, and wasn't afraid to admit it.

"Okay, Tom. My head's spinning now. If you were just starting out with ten head of cattle, what would you feed them?"

Tom roared in laughter. "Well, I'll admit it's like buying a new truck. There's a thousand of 'em on the lot but only one that's just right for what you need.

"If it was me, I'd buy a combination. Do they have good grazing land for the warm weather months?"

"Yes."

"Okay, they'll be used to eating grass, so you'll want to keep them on a similar diet as much as possible. I'd buy two hundred bales of hay. That should get them through a typical winter. I'd also recommend you keep about thirty sacks of compound feed on hand. Give it to them periodically throughout the green season, maybe a couple of scoops every week or so. That'll ensure they get the vitamins and nutrients they need, even if the grass is poor quality.

"Make sure you replenish your feed stock going into the winter. You'll want those thirty sacks standing by in case the winter is extra harsh, or drags on into the springtime.

"Now, then. Do you plan on keeping horses too?"

"I haven't thought of it, to be honest. But I guess I can't be a real cowboy unless I have horses, can I?"

Tom slapped him on the back.

"Now you're talking, partner."

He took Scott to a stack of hay and took out a pair of wire cutters from his back pocket. Then he cut the wires on one of the bales, and pulled off a section of hay from the bale.

"This here's called a flake. Bales come in different sizes, but ours come twelve flakes to a bale. A good sized horse will need one flake in the morning, one flake in the afternoon to keep up his strength. If you work him hard, or if it's particularly cold, feed him three a day instead of two. He'll still need two pounds of feed every day in addition to the hay. That'll keep his innards working so you don't have to flush him out with a garden hose."

Scott pictured himself performing such a task and commented, "I don't think I'd like having to do that."

Tom laughed again and said, "Trust me, partner. The horses don't much like it either."

Scott's mind was racing as he tried to calculate how much he'd need.

"So, two hundred bales and thirty sacks for the cattle, one bale every six days for each horse... oh, hell, just me another two hundred bales for the horses too. It'll get used."

"Atta boy. I saw you pull up with a trailer behind your truck. We can load you up, but it'll take a few trips. Or we can deliver. Anything over two hundred bales, there's no delivery charge."

"Okay, then. If there's no charge, I'll just take my empty trailer on back and let your guys do the haulin'."

"Okay, let's go to the counter and get the paperwork done. Unless there's something else you need."

"Well, as a matter of fact, I'm going to try my hand at raising pigs, chickens and rabbits too."

Tom put his arm around Scott's shoulder and said, "You're my new best friend, little buddy. You just made my truck payment next month for me."

He laughed uproariously.

"Let's go over to the swine and poultry shed and I'll tell you what your options are on the rest of it."

An hour later Scott stood in front of the sales counter as Tom wrote up his sales ticket.

"When's the best day and time to make delivery, Scott?"

"How about Thursday?"

"Thursday it is. Morning or afternoon?"

"Morning is probably better."

"No problem. What's the address?"

"Rural Route 8, Box 54, Junction. I'll draw out a map for your driver."

Tom stopped writing and looked him dead in the eyes, as though disbelieving him.

"Well, I'll be damned. You're the fella who bought the old Ryan place."

"Well yes, yes I am. Did Mr. Ryan buy from you guys also?"

"Yes, sometimes. But mostly I recognized the address because it's almost the same as mine. We're neighbors. I live at Box 58. It's the first house on County Road 7."

Now it was Scott's turn to be surprised.

"The red house with the windmill out front?"

"Yep, that's the one."

"Small world, I guess."

"Yes sir, buddy. Welcome to the neighborhood, and if there's anything I can do to help you get settled into that place of yours, you just let me know. I'd offer to bring you a batch of cookies, but it's just me now. The wife passed several years ago. And trust me, you don't want to be eating anything I make."

Scott reached out his hand and Tom took it.

"Forget the cookies, Tom. I'd rather have a good and friendly neighbor than cookies any day of the week.

Scott walked out of the feed store three thousand dollars lighter than he was when he walked in. But he felt good about it. He was an excellent judge of character, and he knew that Tom Haskins not only gave him a fair deal, but solid advice as well. And he knew they'd not only be good neighbors, but also very good friends.

When they parted ways, Tom shook his hand once again and handed him a piece of paper.

"Tuck that in your wallet, Scott. They don't give working guys like me business cards, but that's got my phone number. You'll find out that there's a lot more to the cattle business than first appears. I've raised stock pretty much all my life, and I'm pretty darn good at it. So anytime you have any questions about the way one of your head is behaving, or anything else, you give me a call. Or hell, just ride up the road and drop in anytime."

"Thanks, Tom. I'll do that."

# -18-

Scott pulled into the compound, and Joyce watched him get out of the truck. She was surprised to see him return with an empty trailer.

"Hey, cowboy! I thought we were going to be stacking hay bales this afternoon! I even brought my muscles today and everything. What's up with that?"

"Well, it turns out I underestimated the amount of hay we'll need. It would have taken me four trips to get everything. So they're going to deliver it the day after tomorrow."

"All right! That means we have the afternoon free. And I know just how we can spend it."

She took his hand and led him to the house, and up the stairs.

"Kick off your boots, cowboy. We've both been working awful hard. Now it's time to have some fun."

That evening over dinner at Perico's, Scott asked, "Do you ride?"

She looked at him and smiled.

"It depends on what you're talking about. You already know I do a pretty good job riding cowboys. I can ride a horse, but I can't ride a motorcycle. Always wanted to learn, though. Why do you ask?"

"I've got an appointment tomorrow with a rancher up near Fredericksburg to look at some horses. Thought I'd take you along so you could pick yours out."

"Why, cowboy, what a great idea. And I'd love to go with you. How many horses are you going to buy?"

"I don't know. I'm thinking two males and three females."

She laughed. "Males and females, huh? Okay. Sounds good to me. But just so the rancher doesn't make too much fun of you, you might want to call them stallions and mares."

Four days later, on Saturday morning, Scott pulled up in his truck with the boys for their usual Saturday morning fence work.

Joyce met them at the truck and asked Scott, "Well, what did they think?"

Jordan looked at his dad.

"Think about what?"

"You didn't tell them, Scott?"

Scott laughed.

"Oh, heck, I forgot. Okay, guys, here's the deal. I'm going to work on the fence today with you. Zachary, this morning I'll help your brother on the fence and Joyce is going to teach you how to ride a horse."

"Cool!"

"And Jordan, this afternoon you and your brother will switch out."

"Cool beans, Dad. Sounds like fun. But... do we still get paid?"

"Yes, you still get paid."

"Well, in that case, count me in. Are you sure you don't want to join us?"

"No, son. That's pretty much all I've been doing for the last three days. My butt is sore enough already."

Scott and Jordan spent the morning putting up fence panels. During a break, they each drank a bottle of cold water and paced off the fence line that still needed to be done.

"Great. At the rate you guys are going, four more weekends and you'll be done."

"And then what?"

"What do you mean, son?"

"I mean, do you have any other jobs we can do around here on the weekends? Or am I going to have to flip burgers somewhere?"

"Oh, I wouldn't worry much about that. There will always be work around here to keep you guys busy on the weekends. I thought for your next project you can learn how to drive the Bobcat and dig out the pond."

"Seriously? That sounds a lot more fun than hanging up fence panels. But what do you mean, dig out the pond?"

"Well, the pond is too small and too shallow. If we had a bad drought it would dry up and kill all the fish. We need to triple its size and make it a lot deeper."

"How do we do that?"

"Simple. We put you on the Bobcat with a bucket on the front, and you dig out a very large hole in the ground adjacent to the present pond. One bucket at a time. You drag the bucket along the ground until the bucket is full. Then you tilt it back and haul the dirt away."

"Haul it to where?"

"To the perimeter of the property. You'll take it to the edge of the property and dump it. Then the next load, you'll dump next to the load before it. You'll go all the way around the property and build a twelve inch berm."

"Why?"

"To keep the rainwater in. That way if the stream that runs through the property ever dries up, or gets diverted by somebody upstream and no longer feeds the pond, we can do it with rainwater instead.

"The berm will make sure that all of the rain that falls within the property stays here. It won't run off and go somewhere else. A lot of it, of course, will soak into the ground, and that's okay. It'll help grow our crops and the grass for the cattle to eat.

"But when the rainfall is heavy, and rains more than the ground needs, we'll divert the extra into the pond. And there should be enough rainfall over the course of the year to keep the pond full. But like I said, if we ever have a drought, the fish may not survive unless the pond is a lot deeper."

"Okay, but how do we make the rainwater standing in puddles on one end of the property go to the other end where the pond is?"

"Oh, it'll take some time, but basically we'll make a series of channels and waterways."

Jordan gave him a puzzled look. He obviously didn't understand.

"Okay. We're going to make a concrete drag. We'll take a five gallon bucket, fill it with concrete, and stick an upside down u-bolt in the center of it, with just the "u" sticking out of the concrete

"After it dries, we'll cut the bucket away and we'll have a big, rough, hundred pound chunk of concrete that we'll be able to tie a long chain onto so we can drag it around."

"Okay. Then what?"

"Then we just wait until we have a heavy rain. After the rain, I'll go out with some three foot wooden stakes with orange surveyor's tape tied to the end. You can go with me to help, in fact.

"We'll walk over the whole property, and everywhere there is a significant puddle of standing water, we'll put a stake into the ground at what appears to be the deepest part of the puddle.

"Then, a couple of days later..."

Jordan held up his hand to stop his father.

"Wait. I think I've got it. A couple of days later after the ground isn't quite so muddy, we take the chunk of concrete to where the stake is, and we drag the concrete from there to the fishing pond."

"Exactly. The concrete won't make a very deep rut. Maybe six to eight inches. But it will give the puddle a channel to run off to after the next rainfall. And it'll probably take several big rainfalls to get the runoffs just right. But eventually, all the rain that doesn't soak into the ground within half an hour to an hour will be channeled toward the pond."

"Okay. So tell me again how I'm going to dig out the pond without drowning in the water that's already there."

"Simple. You use the Bobcat to dig a second pond. It will be adjacent to the existing pond, but they won't be connected. We'll leave maybe twelve to fifteen feet of space between them. After the deeper part is dug, we'll divert the stream to fill it up, and the two will join to become one big pond."

"I've been meaning to ask you, Dad, are there any fish in the pond now?"

"Oh, yeah. Joyce and I went fishing down there a few weeks ago while you were in school. We caught a freshwater perch and a couple of good sized catfish. I'm going to bring in some live crawdads too, and I'm thinking the stream we're going to divert probably has some trout in it too."

"Dad, can I ask you something? Man to man?"

"Sure, son. What is it?"

"This big blackout thing. Are you positive it's going to happen? I mean, you're going through an awful lot of work to get this place ready. What if it never happens?"

"Well, the answer to your first question is yes. I'm pretty positive it's going to happen. I just don't know when, but I think it's going to be fairly soon. But I would love to be wrong. And if I am wrong… if it never happens, then there's not a lot of harm done. One of you, either you or Zach, will have a hell of a vacation home to spend your weekends. Of course, y'all can duke it out amongst yourselves after I'm gone to see who gets it.

"Because even if I am wrong, I plan to live here anyway for the rest of my days."

# -19-

It was about nine p.m. the following Monday when Scott pulled into Linda's driveway to pick up the boys.

He knew immediately that something was wrong. He didn't even get a chance to turn off the ignition when the boys came bounding out of the house. That was unusual, because they were never ready to go when he showed up.

In addition, they were sullen and quiet. Zachary didn't even respond when Scott said hello.

Scott looked at the front of the house, expecting to see Linda standing there, as she always was when they left, waving goodbye to them.

Instead, the front door was closed and Linda was nowhere in sight.

He looked at Jordan, sitting in the front seat beside him.

"Jordan, what in hell is going on?"

Jordan looked down. He hesitated, and said, "I'm not allowed to say."

Scott looked in the back seat at Zachary. Zachary looked down also. Both boys hated keeping secrets from their father. But they were sworn to secrecy.

Scott turned off the ignition and stepped out of the truck, leaving his boys behind.

Zachary asked his brother, "What do you think he'll do?"

Jordan answered, "I don't know, Zach. I just hope he doesn't have his gun in the glove box."

Scott rang the bell, but no one answered. He tried the door and it was unlocked. Jordan had left it that way on purpose. He knew his father well.

Scott went through the house calling Linda's name, and finally found her lying in bed, badly beaten.

He flew into a sudden rage.

"Where is that son of a bitch? I'll kill him, I swear to God!"

"Scott, no! It wasn't his fault, I swear it wasn't. I brought it on myself."

He tenderly touched her face. And as gentle as his touch was, she still winced from the pain. Both of her eyes were blackened. One was almost swollen closed. She had a cut across the bridge of her nose, and her upper lip was badly swollen. Her left cheek sported a nasty bruise.

"Tell me what happened."

"Scott, it was my fault, I swear. I sassed him. I shouldn't have, I know. I know how he gets when he's drunk. I should have held my tongue. But I sassed him by asking him where he'd been. It was my fault, not his."

"When is he coming back?"

"Probably not until morning."

"Is the rest of your body beaten too?"

"Some. But nothing's broken, near as I can tell."

"Okay. I'm going to send the boys back in here to pack your things. You're getting out of here."

"But Scott, how is he going to get by without me to cook and do things for him? He can't live without me around."

"That's the plan."

"But…"

"But nothing. You need to get away from that animal before he goes too far and kills you some night. Is that what you want?"

"No. You know I don't. But you don't understand. He gets frustrated, you know? It's hard for him to find work, with his record and all. And when he does find a job, they ride him without mercy until he has to quit or says something that gets him fired. And then he gets drunk to drown his sorrows."

"Jesus Christ! He got fired *again?*"

"Yes. But it wasn't his fault. Where will I go?"

"Right. It's never his fault. You're coming up to the compound. You're going to stay there from now on. And I hope you didn't tell him where it's at. Because if he so much as steps one foot on my property I swear I'll blow him into a hundred pieces."

With that, he stormed out of the room and went out to the boys.

"Go back in and help your mother pack, boys. We're moving her the hell away from here."

The gloom and doom on his sons' faces disappeared. Jordan said, "Hoo-rah!" and gave his younger brother a high five.

Scott pulled out his cell phone to make a phone call he didn't expect to be much fun. How was he going to tell his present girlfriend that he was moving his ex-wife in with them?

He dialed Joyce's number with the dread of a condemned man being strapped into Old Sparky.

# -20-

As it turned out, Joyce was pleased as punch to hear that Linda was moving into the compound. Scott had underestimated her.

"I think it's a great idea, Scott. I mean, we were planning on bringing her in when the blackout hit anyway. This way it'll give us a chance to ease into it without being rushed."

"I didn't think you'd want her invading your territory any sooner than she had to."

"Damn, Scott. You know me better than that. I am not threatened by any woman. And I'm not jealous of any woman either. Unless you say you're bringing her into our bedroom, I have no qualms with her being at the compound. And by the way, if you do ever invite her into our bedroom, we'll have the sweetest tomatoes in ten counties and you'll be the fertilizer. Understand?"

He smiled. He liked Joyce's feisty side.

"Understand."

"And besides, honey, I've been beaten by men before too. I know what she's going through. You were right in pulling her out of there. Some women just don't have the gumption to make that move on their own. They have to be pushed."

Late that night, close to midnight, Scott pulled his truck into the compound. Jordan followed behind them in his mother's car.

They went inside and showed Linda to the guest room.

"Make yourself at home. Since it's late, I'm going to let the boys stay here for the night. Whatever you need, let them get it for you. You need to stay in bed until you recover and the soreness goes away."

"But how will I get to and from work once I'm healed?"

"Tomorrow I'll draw you a map to get back to the highway. Once you're back on Highway 83, getting back to the interstate is easy. All you have to do is leave forty five minutes earlier than you're used to."

"Can I at least call Glen and tell him I'm okay and not to worry about me?"

"You can call anyone you want. I don't understand why you're so worried about him, though. He obviously doesn't give a damn about you."

"You just don't know him like I do, Scott. You don't understand him."

"You're right. I don't understand any man who would beat a woman. Just remember one thing, Linda. I meant what I said. If he dares to show his face up here I will rip him to shreds, so help me God."

Linda decided not to call Glen. She'd warned him enough times over the previous few months that she would leave him if he didn't change his ways. By morning she was finally feeling strong enough to survive without him.

Joyce arrived early the following morning, and she and Linda had a long heart to heart. About men, about the situation at the compound, about a thousand other things. By the time Scott and the boys got out of bed, the ladies had had a good chance to bond.

It turned out that any fears of drama Scott had were unfounded. The two women had many more things in common than they had differences. And they were becoming fast friends.

Scott stood at the kitchen stove, cracking oily eggs into a frying pan, and asked Linda how she felt.

"Sore. But somehow, despite the bruises, I slept better here last night than I would have at home. I don't know why, but I did."

"I know exactly why," Joyce added. "Because deep down inside you knew you were safe here. So your body was able to relax. You didn't have to worry about whether you'd be his punching bag again when you woke up in the morning."

"Yes, you're probably right."

Scott asked, "So, what did you two talk about before I got here?"

"Oh, anything and everything. Girl stuff mostly."

Joyce winked at Linda and continued, "And we compared notes. You know, all of your shortcomings in bed. That kind of thing."

Scott turned and glared and Linda laughed out loud. Then she winced when she found out too late that laughing hurt her swollen lip.

"She's just kidding, goober. Actually, we were talking about putting in the garden out back. Turns out we both love to garden. So we're going seed shopping while you he-men are doing all the he-man stuff around here today."

"Yeah, well I don't know how much work I'll get out of the other he-men. They told me they were up until 3 a.m. playing video games."

"I was wondering why they haven't come downstairs yet."

"If they went back to bed I'm going to go up there with a spray bottle full of ice water."

"Well, that'll certainly get their attention."

"Scott, how much of the front part of the compound did you plan for our vegetable garden?

The western half. Actually, it can creep over into the eastern half if you want. Just don't crowd it out too much. We'll still need to get vehicles in and out of there, to get hay and feed and stuff to the barns.

And I'm going to order another Butler building and have it delivered next week.

"Really? How come? We've got places for all the tools and feed and stuff now."

"It's for Jordan. He gave me the old 'Dad, I will be an adult soon, I will need to move out on my own' speech the other day."

"Oh, really? And what did you tell him?"

"I told him I'd bring in an extra building. It'll be about the size of a two car garage. Just the right size for a bachelor pad. And I told him I'd buy all the building materials we'd need to run power and plumbing to it and to fix it up real nice. And that after the power went out and we all came to live up here, that it would be our little project. Mine and his. And that we would work together to make him a nice apartment to live in."

"And what did he say?"

"He thought it was a great idea."

"Well, so do I. It'll give the two of you a chance to bond."

"Yep. And after the blackout happens, I suspect one of the things that will drive us most crazy is boredom. I mean, we won't be able to just jump in a car and go places anymore. No movies, no restaurants, no bowling alleys or nightclubs. We're all going to be looking for things to occupy our spare time. And that project will keep Jordan and I busy for several months.

"I'm actually kinda looking forward to it."

# -21-

It was a miserable and chilly day when Scott pulled into the yard and started offloading the panels of two very large wire cages.

Linda and Joyce were already standing outside, looking up at the sky.

"Hey, you two. What's up?"

"Oh, not much. We were trying to decide whether to go ahead with our plans to plant our garden today. What do you think?"

Scott looked up at the dark clouds swirling slowly overhead.

"I don't know. The weather forecast didn't say anything about a storm coming in. But it sure looks to me like one's on the way."

"Yeah. That's what we thought. If course, if we got the seeds in the ground before the storm hit, the rain could water them for us."

"Yeah, or if it was too heavy, it could wash all your seeds away, and then you'd have to start all over again."

Joyce looked at Linda and asked, "What do you think?"

"I think we shouldn't risk it. There are plenty of other chores we can do inside today. Let's save the planting for tomorrow and finish up the canning instead."

Scott looked at Linda and said, "Hey, it just occurred to me, since when are you off on Mondays?"

"Since I took a week's vacation to get the garden planted."

"Well, that didn't work out too well for you, now did it?"

"Hey, what's with the big cage? Is that a 'time-out' jail for the boys?"

"Nope. These are rabbit cages. Two of them. They're going out there under the shed I built next to the chicken coup."

"I was wondering what you were going to put under there."

"Well now you know. Y'all wanna help?"

"Sure. Why not? But why two cages? And why rabbits? I thought you told the boys we weren't bringing any pets into the compound."

"One cage is for three boy rabbits. The other cage is for three girl rabbits."

"Oh, now that's just cruel, Scott. So they can look at each other but can't have any romance?"

"Oh, once the blackout happens, they'll get plenty of romance. That's when we let them out into the yard and they can do what rabbits do best. And they're not pets, by the way. They're going to be a big part of our diet"

"We're going to eat the cute little bunnies?"

"Yep. We'll keep them separated until we need them to multiply. Then once they start mingling, these six can produce two to three hundred offspring a year. They'll be about the size of a chicken, just as easy to prepare, and will have even more protein."

"Just as long as you kill them and skin them, Scott. I don't think I could bring myself to do it."

"Wow, so we'll have rabbits, pigs, chickens and cows. We need to put a sign out front that says 'Scott's Zoo.' Maybe we can charge admission."

"Don't forget the horses."

Joyce looked at Linda.

"Speaking of horses... Linda, you mentioned that you never learned to ride. Is that something you want to learn today? We can start your first lesson this morning since we can't plant the garden."

"No, thank you. I've lived this long without knowing how to ride a smelly old horse. No sense learning how now."

Scott said, "Speaking of horses, Joyce, I noticed yesterday that Trigger's still got two flakes of hay in his stall. Any idea why he's not eating?"

"No, I don't have a clue. I noticed the same thing. I know if he doesn't eat, it'll only take a couple of days for him to start getting weak. Should we get the vet out here to take a look at him?"

"Not yet. I've got a friend I made at the feed store awhile back who lives right up the road. I'll give him a call and see if he can drop by after he gets off work. He seems to know a lot about livestock and I want the two of you to meet him anyway."

They had just finished assembling the rabbit cages beneath the shed when the clouds opened up and it started raining. The three ran for cover in the house.

"Looks like you made a good call on not planting today."

"Of course. We're women, Good calls are the only ones we make. So we'll be canning today. Would you like to help?"

"No, thanks, I'll pass. As soon as the rain stops I'm going to start bringing in plywood to reinforce the outer walls. I've got my own mission to accomplish."

# -22-

A little after five p.m., Tom Haskins pulled into the yard in an old red Ram pickup.

"Well, howdy there, neighbor. How y'all doing?"

"Doing very well, Tom. I appreciate you stopping by. Want to come inside for some iced tea, and to meet everybody else?"

"Sure thing. Iced tea sounds real good."

Scott and Tom walked into the kitchen where the girls were canning peaches. They had a peach cobbler baking in the oven, and its sweet aroma wafted throughout the house.

"Sure smells sweeter than my place, I'll tell you what."

"Tom, this is my girlfriend Joyce, and my ex wife and one of my oldest friends Linda."

"Hey, watch the way you say 'oldest.'"

Both women shook Tom's outstretched hand. Linda held onto it just a tad bit longer than was necessary. It didn't escape the notice of Tom, or of Joyce, who raised an eyebrow and smiled.

"Tom, do you like your tea sweet or unsweet?"

"Sweet, please. Texas style."

Linda dropped two teaspoons of sugar into his glass and stirred it.

Tom looked at Scott and said, "So, tell me about your pony that's ailin'."

"His name's Trigger. Usually eats like a horse, if you'll pardon the bad pun. The last two or three days, though, he's just been picking at his feed. And not eating much of his hay at all."

"Is he drinking plenty of water, and is his belly extended?"

"I hadn't noticed either. Is that important?"

"Yep. Those are the first two things to watch for when a pony stops eating. He's probably just stove up is all. It happens sometimes, and we can fix it if that's all it is. Is he the one you're using to teach your boys to ride?"

"No, the boys are learning on Sally. She's a bit more gentle."

"And how are they coming?"

"So far, real well."

Linda spoke up.

"Someday I hope to learn to ride too. I've always wanted to learn, but nobody's ever really offered to teach me."

Joyce almost choked on her iced tea, but didn't say anything. Instead she stole a glance at Scott, who winked at her.

Tom, who was as much a Texas gentleman as he was a friendly neighbor, looked at Linda and said, "Well shoot, lovely lady. I'll teach you how to ride myself if you want to come by and visit this weekend. I live at the end of the road. Scott knows where it is. I've got an old mare named Goldilocks who's just as gentle as they come. She'll take you on a slow gallop so smooth you can take your iced tea along and won't spill a drop."

"Well, thank you, Tom. That sounds like fun. Are you sure you won't mind?"

"No, not at all. As long as you don't mind my place too much. It's just me and my dog Red now, and it's… well, it's a might dusty and disorganized. Hasn't had a woman's touch in awhile, you see."

"Oh, that won't bother me a bit. I'll make plans to come and see you on Saturday, then. And you be sure and come back in here after you look at that old horse so I can serve you up some peach cobbler."

The men finished their iced tea and headed out to the stable to look at Trigger. As soon as they stepped out the door, Joyce looked at Linda with her mouth wide open.

Linda said, "What? You've got a man of your own. Maybe I want one too. And did you see the size of his hands?"

They both burst out laughing.

"Oh, trust me, girlfriend. I noticed. He's got big feet too, if that counts for anything."

"Well, I'll let you know after the weekend is up."

"You're a shameful hussy, you know that?"

"Yep. I know. You say that like it's a bad thing."

An hour later the men walked back into the house and washed up in the back lavatory. Trigger's innards had been flushed out with a water hose, and while they were at it the pair took a look at all the other livestock. Everything looked healthy, and Tom commented that Scott got a great deal on his cattle.

"Prime beef. Them cattle will make some good eatin' when you're ready for 'em. Have you done any butchering before?"

"No, sir. Never have, and it's not something I'm looking forward to."

"Hell, it's a piece of cake. Whenever you've got one that's ready to butcher, just let me know. I'll show you how to kill it without spoiling the meat. Then I'll show you how to butcher it. Once you do it once or twice, you'll be surprised how easy it is. Same for the pigs."

Scott noticed Linda staring at Tom's hands as he spoke. Joyce, in turn, was staring intently at Linda and giggling.

"What's so funny?" he asked, as Linda and Joyce both burst out laughing.

"Oh, nothing. Just an inside joke. Nothing to concern yourself about. Are you boys ready for some cobbler?"

"Don't mind if I do."

"Sure, why not?"

Tom cranked up his truck half an hour later and pulled out of the drive. The rest of the group walked him out into the yard, and the girls waved goodbye to him.

Scott said, "Well, I guess I'd better get to the house myself and pick up the boys. Have y'all got plans for supper, or do you want to go out?"

Joyce and Linda looked at each other. They had been so sidetracked with the canning and with the size of Tom's hands that neither of them had even thought about starting dinner.

Joyce said, "Hold on. Let me make sure everything's turned off and get our bags."

They crawled into Scott's truck and picked up the boys from the house. Then they went to Mamacita's Restaurant on

I-10 in San Antonio and feasted on some magnificent Mexican food.

Over dinner, Scott casually asked the girls what they thought of their new neighbor.

Joyce said, "Ask Linda. I think she's smitten with him."

Linda didn't deny the charge.

"I like him. I like him a lot."

## -23-

Jordan walked into the back bedroom to find his father sitting at a desk in front of a ham radio.

"Ten-four, good buddy. You got a copy on that, Pig Pen? You got that convoy in motion, stayin' ahead of that old Smokey the Bear?"

Scott took the headphones off his ears and laid them on the desk in front of him. He turned around and looked his oldest son in the eye.

"Have you been smoking crack?"

Jordan laughed.

"Isn't that the way you old timers talked back in the CB radio days? You know, back when those things were popular and all?"

Now it was Scott's turn to laugh.

"Oh, the ignorance of youth. Sit down, my boy, and let me educate you."

Jordan sat down.

"First of all, this is not a CB radio. It's a ham radio."

"Okay. So what's the difference?"

"CB radios are mobile. Portable. Made for vehicles to communicate with each other and with their base stations. Like walkie talkies on steroids. They have a range of just a few miles. This, on the other hand, can reach around the world. I was just carrying on a conversation with a man in Sydney, Australia."

"Wow, no shit?"

Scott raised an eyebrow.

"Sorry, Dad. No kidding?"

"No kidding, son. The radio waves bounce off satellites just like overseas phone calls. So you can talk to anyone, anywhere."

"Cool. So why do we have one?"

"Once the power goes out and we move up here, we won't venture out. There won't be any more TV or radio to tell us what's going on out there. The only way we'll be able to communicate is by ham radio. And that's also the only way we'll know what's going on in the world."

"And that's important why, again?"

"Because I'm hoping that after a few years the world can find ways to recover. I personally think it'll take generations. But since it'll really be the only thing the world is working on, maybe they can put their heads together and find ways of restoring the electrical grids and replacing all the shorted out electronics."

"So we'll know if it's ever safe to come out and rejoin the rest of the world?"

"Exactly."

"Okay, Dad. I know I'm not the smartest guy in the world, but…"

Scott smiled and asked, "Ya think?"

Jordan playfully punched his father on the arm and continued.

"If everything else in the world that runs on electricity gets ruined by the EMPs, then isn't it true that this thing won't work either?"

"Actually, Jordan, that's a very good question. It shows you're using your head. That's good. And you're right. This would be ruined like everything else. If it was unprotected. But it'll be in the Foley box like all the other things we need to protect. So will the transceiver at the top of the antenna tower. I just pulled this out to test it, and to spread the word to a few other ham operators around the country."

"What did you tell them?"

"I told them that I had an excellent and very qualified scientific source who believes that the world will be bombarded by EMPs in the very near future. I told them that when it happens, the only way to spread news around the country and world is by using ham radios that were protected from the EMPs. And I encouraged them to protect their equipment so that it wouldn't be ruined."

"How many of them thought you were crazy?"

"A few did. But I was surprised at how many didn't."

"Really?"

"Yep. You have to remember that ham radio users are kind of a rebellious bunch. A good portion of them do not trust governments, and think that society will eventually fall into chaos. Some of them are what are called preppers. People who believe the world, or society, is going to collapse in various ways, and are preparing for when that happens."

"Like us."

"Yes. Just like us. And also not like us. You see, most of them have never heard of EMPs. They think the breakdown of society is coming because terrorists get their hands on Russia's nuclear bombs and start using them on us. Or because the economy collapses into chaos. Or because global warming causes a series of really bad natural disasters. Or any one of a number of other things.

"And it doesn't really matter what their beliefs are, as long as they are taking measures to survive. All I want to do is talk them into taking measures to preserve their radios and a power source so we can communicate and share information after the shit hits the fan."

"How come you can say shit and I can't?"

"Because I'm an adult. You're still a snotty nosed kid."

"Dad, can I ask you something that's completely unrelated to ham radios and the end of the world and stuff?"

"Sure. What is it?"

"Mom is getting pretty serious about this Tom guy. They've gone out like six or eight times this month. Do you think she's getting serious enough to marry him or something?"

"Would it bother you if she did?"

"I don't know. I mean, he seems like a nice guy and all. And they really seem to like each other. It's just that, I don't know. I'm tired of seeing her getting beaten up and stuff. And she has terrible taste when it comes to picking out men."

Scott feigned anger.

"Hey, boy! She chose me, you know."

"You know what I mean, Dad. Men since you. Nearly every one of the men she's dated has taken advantage of her or beaten her or stolen from her. And sometimes all three."

"I wouldn't worry about it, son, for several reasons. First of all, I met Tom before she did. And I'm an excellent judge of character. Tom struck me as a good and honorable man. He's a protector, not an abuser. I felt that from the beginning and I still believe it. And I wouldn't have introduced him to your mother if I hadn't believed that.

"Second, she's a good woman and she's got a good head on her shoulders. When she went looking for men before, it was because she was lonely. But since she's been up here I've noticed a change in her. With all of us sharing the same house, she's not lonely anymore. And I don't want to use the word desperate, but I'll say this. I don't see her in such a hurry to need a man anymore. I think it finally dawned on her that she can do just fine without a man.

"And I think it changed her whole perspective on things. Yes, she went after Tom. But I think she knows now that she doesn't have to settle for just any man who comes along just because she's lonely. I think she realizes now that if Tom is flawed, that she can just tell him to get lost. That she's okay without him. And that puts her in a way more powerful position than she ever was in before."

"I suppose. I just hope you're right."

"Of course I'm right."

Jordan laughed.

"But how do you know?"

"Because I'm a father. And fathers are always right."

# -24-

By the end of the summer, everything was coming along quite nicely. The compound was about ninety percent complete, everyone was getting along famously, and all things were running smoothly.

There were only two projects still to be done. And one was nearing its final stages.

Jordan had been digging out the deep end of the pond for five months, eight hours each Saturday and eight hours each Sunday. When school let out for the summer, he worked Monday, Tuesday and Wednesday too.

Scott wasn't a total slave driver, though. He paid his son well, and with that pay, Jordan was able to entertain his new girlfriend Sara in grand style.

The work on the pond was monotonous, and Jordan had become bored with it months before.

There was nothing hard about it either. He drove to the pond site in the Bobcat and dropped the bucket so that it scraped along the ground as he drove forward.

Once the bucket was filled, he drove to the perimeter of the property and dumped his load, alongside the load he'd dumped just twelve minutes before. By doing so, he was killing two birds with one stone. He was greatly increasing the size of the pond and making the new half much deeper to allow the fish to grow in numbers and to grow to larger sizes. And the berm he was building would be grown over with grass and become a permanent feature of the land. During rainstorms it would prevent runoff, keeping all the water that fell on their property from running elsewhere. Instead, it would soak into the ground or run into their fishing pond.

Day by day, load by load, Jordan slowly accomplished his mission. He was looking forward to the day his dad said "enough" and they started filling the pond. That's when he'd feel the pride of ownership for the project, and get to stand back and admire what he'd accomplished.

Scott's younger son Zachary was helping his dad with the other unfinished project. It was grunt work, pure and simple, but Zach was strong for his age and wanting to grow stronger. And Scott was certainly willing to help him attain that particular goal.

The pair carried plywood into the house and up the stairs, a single sheet at a time. They started at the northeast corner of the house, laying down four sheets of half inch plywood in a stack. Then they lifted up all four sheets, and installed wooden stops in the floor and the ceiling to hold them into place.

Joyce and Linda, out of curiosity, went up the stairs to see what they were doing.

"I'm bulletproofing the house," Scott answered.

"You're doing *what?*"

"I'm bulletproofing the house."

He explained his logic.

"There may well come a time when we have to defend what's ours. And it could get pretty ugly."

"What do you mean?"

"I mean that even in the best of times, there's a certain type of man who finds it easier to just take from someone else instead of work for what he needs. In the worst of times, when the whole world is scrambling to survive, I expect there'll be a lot more of that type of men out there.

"That's one of the main reasons we're so isolated. Without vehicles, we'll be a lot harder to get to than, say, if we were closer to town.

"There aren't a lot of people who will walk seventy miles in search of safety and to find food and shelter."

His next sentence bore an ominous tone.

"But some will."

"And you think they'll attack us?"

"I think some might. I think it'll depend on how curious they are."

He went on to explain.

"I think there will be some men, and maybe their families too, who leave San Antonio in search of someplace safer, where maybe they can hunt deer and rabbits for food, and maybe even grow a garden. Most of them will find a place to settle before they get to this point. But gradually, I think some will have to come this far because the closer places are taken.

"And if they happen to be looking for a place to settle, and see our big black fence off in the distance, some might be curious enough to want to see what's inside our fence. And if they can see what's inside our fence, they're surely going to want it.

"And some of them might even be bold enough to try to take it."

"But we've got the high ground here, Scott. There aren't any hills close enough to see into our compound, and there's too many trees in the way."

Scott shook his head.

"They don't need any hills."

He took the women to the window of the upstairs bedroom they were in. They looked out the window to the east.

The women had forgotten about the string of high tension power lines that ran past the compound two hundred yards to the east, and continued up north to the power plant outside of Kerrville. Each tower stood as tall as a twenty story building, and were spaced exactly one hundred fifty yards apart.

Joyce said, "Dammit! You think they'll climb the towers?"

"I would," Scott said, "if I were in their situation. If I was looking for a safe place to settle, I'd climb up one of the towers every mile or two just to have a look, to see if there was a clearing near a stream, or maybe an abandoned farmhouse. And if I saw a big black fence with a garden and a herd of cattle inside it, I just might want it bad enough to try to take it."

"How hard is it to climb one of those towers?"

"Oh, it's easy as can be. The only reason people don't climb them now, for the fun of it, is because not many men will climb a steel tower with two inch thick power lines buzzing above them, carrying fifty thousand volts. But once they're dead, it's no different than climbing a tree. In fact, it's easier, because the towers have steel ladders attached to them. Trees don't."

"Okay. I almost wish you hadn't told me. But since you did, what's our plan to protect ourselves?"

"That's where the plywood comes in. We're going to panel the whole interior of the house with four sheets of plywood. And it's simple to install. All we do is stand up four sheets against the wall, and install a wooden strip on the floor and the ceiling to hold them into place. When we're done, we'll have a two inch thick wall to catch bullets, in addition to the brick and outer and inner walls of the house."

"Will that be enough?"

"It should be. I stood up four sheets against one of the barns the other day while you were all gone and fired some AR-15 rounds and 9 millimeter rounds into it. Nothing got past the third sheet. And that didn't take into consideration the other layers from the house itself."

"You're not going to board over the windows, are you?"

"No, but I've got a plan for the windows too. Initially we'll cover the walls but leave the windows uncovered. Then we'll go back and build portable walls. They'll be four sheets of plywood thick, but will be on wheels. They'll roll off to one side when not in use, and will stay in place by rails on the floor and ceiling. I'll make a shooting slot in each one about four inches high and a foot wide. That way we can shoot back if we're fired upon. We'll be able to roll the portable walls into place within seconds if we ever need them."

Joyce was impressed.

"Wow, you're one smart cookie, mister."

"That's not all. Once the power goes out, the electric company will abandon those power lines. For one thing, they won't need them any more. The power station will be out of commission permanently. And for another thing, none of their vehicles will work, so they couldn't patrol the area around the lines even if they wanted to."

"So what are you planning to do?"

"Two things. First of all, I'm going to take some wireless long-distance cameras and mount one pointed in each direction, so we can see anyone following the power lines either up or down the mountain. The cameras are already in the Foley cage, so they'll still work after the blackout. And they'll work with small solar panels, like a lot of the portable highway signs they use these days. They will have attached batteries that will never go dead unless we have about three consecutive days without sunshine.

"The second thing I plan to do is take my sixteen foot ladder and a cutting torch and cut the ladders off the towers. They can still get up there, but they'll have to jump sixteen feet to grab onto something. My guess is they'll just pass it on by."

"How many towers will you have to do that to?"

"Only six. I climbed to the top of the wind turbine to service it a couple of months ago. It's a lot taller than the fence. While I was up there I looked out at the towers. There were only six of them where I could see the lower half of the towers above the trees. The rest of them are okay. If we can't see the lower half, then anyone on the lower half won't be able to see us either."

"There's one last thing, but I'll only use it as a last resort."

"What's that?"

"The cameras will be attached to a motion sensor alarm. We'll know when someone is coming long before they get here. And we'll see if they start trying to climb the towers. I'll have plenty of time to set up my sniper rifle and zero in on them."

"You'd shoot them off the tower?"

"Yes, and here's why. A normal man will pass by the tower when he sees the ladder's been cut away. He'll just keep going until he finds another one that has a ladder. That's if all he's looking for is a safe place to stay.

"If he goes through all the effort of getting up on a tower with no ladder, then he's out for more than just safety for himself. If he's curious enough and devious enough to force himself up that tower to see what we're hiding, then he's a threat to us. And I'll take him out in a heartbeat."

"My God, Scott. Don't tell me you're serious. What if he's got his family with him? Are you going to just shoot him off the tower in front of his children?"

Scott was stumped. That didn't happen often, because he usually thought things thoroughly through. But it had never occurred to him he might have to shoot a man in front of his loved ones.

He knew he'd have to put some more thought into this part of his plan.

He muttered, "Let's just hope it doesn't come to that."

## -25-

Joyce stopped and got an Egg McMuffin on her way to the office. She had planned on making breakfast at home before she met a client in Northridge Estates to show a house. But then she remembered she left the sales packet for the house sitting on her desk the day before.

"Dammit," she murmured under her breath. She hated it when she did stupid things. Luckily, the office wasn't too far out of the way.

She'd have to forego a leisurely breakfast, but if traffic wasn't too bad she'd have a few minutes to eat at her desk.

Traffic wasn't bad, and when she got to the register at McDonald's and ordered her sandwich, she was greeted with a smile by the manager.

"Good morning, ma'am. We're running a new promotion this week, and every hundredth customer gets breakfast on us. No charge for you today."

Joyce didn't know what to say. She'd never known McDonald's to give anything away free.

She managed, "Um, thank you..." and grabbed her breakfast and headed for the door.

Traffic the rest of the way to the office was extraordinarily light. She began to think that maybe this was her lucky day after all. The house she was showing was a four million dollar estate. If she could secure the sale she'd lock up a nice commission. Yes. Today was her lucky day. She could feel it in her bones.

She sat down at her desk and put the sales packet on top of her car keys. No way was she going to walk out the door without it a second time.

The clock said 10:17. She could leave at 10:30 and still make it to the house with twenty minutes to spare. She'd learned years before that although prospective buyers are almost always late, realtors should always be a bit early. There's always a scuffed floor to wipe, or litter in the yard. Or some other little thing that'll turn a buyer off.

She eased back in her chair and took a bite of her Egg McMuffin.

The fluorescent lights above her head flickered and then went off.

"Damn power surge."

Someone in the outer office said, "Damn! I just lost my monthly report!"

The office smart aleck shouted out, "Two words: Auto Save."

Joyce sat back and relaxed. The power would be back on in a minute or two. The building they were in was old, and this happened on a regular basis, every time the weather was stormy. It always came back on rather quickly.

She took another bite of her sandwich, careful not to drop anything on her jacket in the semi-darkness.

While chewing, it dawned on her. Wait a minute. It's not stormy today. Not even windy. Then what in heck made the power go out?

In the outer office, somebody shouted, "Hey! Look out the window!"

Joyce got up from her desk, walked to the window, and pulled the heavy gold curtain aside.

The street outside looked like a parking lot. As far as she could see in both directions, cars and trucks were stopped dead in their tracks. Several of them had their hoods up, and their drivers were checking their engines, wiggling battery cables, messing with carburetors.

And scratching their heads.

Several of them were standing outside their cars, pacing back and forth, talking to other motorists or trying to call a loved one for a ride, or for a tow truck.

Trying to call, but not being able to.

Joyce saw three different people punching at their telephones, then looking at them disgustedly. One woman was so disgusted that her phone didn't work, she threw it to the ground.

Off in the distance, she heard a baby cry. Then she heard a woman scream and point to the sky.

Joyce looked in the direction the woman was pointing, as did several other people.

A low flying commercial airliner was approaching them from the east, no more than five hundred feet off the ground. It looked like it was gently gliding in for a landing.

But the nearest airport was miles away.

The airplane flew silently over them, with no working engines, so closely that Joyce could see the faces of panicked passengers looking out the windows. It continued on, deathly quiet, until it crashed in a fireball at a large apartment complex a quarter of a mile away.

There were more screams outside. And more crying.

Instinctively, Joyce reached for her cell phone to call 911. Deep inside, though, she knew it was not working. Her cell phone, her lifeline to the world, was now nothing more than a worthless paperweight.

The solar storm had hit. The blackout had begun.

# -26-

Zachary was in third period. Eighth grade algebra. He couldn't stand algebra, and he hated Mr. Jenkins. Mr. Jenkins was a turd with ears. No, wait. He didn't have that much personality.

Zach hated the class. He hated the teacher. The only thing good about coming to this room every morning, the only thing that made sitting here tolerable, was that he sat directly behind Amy Alvord.

He'd been madly and deeply in love with Amy since the first grade. He was convinced that someday they'd marry. Of course, the odds were against it, since he'd never mustered the courage to say more than a few words to her.

It wasn't that he was afraid to talk to her. It was just that, well, she was so beautiful and wonderful and popular. And Zachary was just... Zachary.

In his early years, he convinced himself that someday he'd get the nerve to talk to her. And after awhile he'd become bold enough to ask her to be his girlfriend. And in his fantasy world, of course, she'd say yes. And that would lead to the pair going steady, and then being college sweethearts, and then getting married and having a zillion kids.

The trouble was, as each year went by, Amy became more and more unapproachable. As she grew into a beautiful teenager, she attracted more and more attention from other boys. And that got exponentially worse at the start of the previous school year, when she was one of the few girls to start wearing a bra. And one of a vastly fewer number who actually needed one.

Suddenly Amy was the center of attention among the football team and the preppies in the school. And poor Zachary was pushed even farther into the background.

Since his dad had told him months before about the world going black some day, and about Zachary having to move away, he started to feel a certain desperation. He just could not go on with his life without letting Amy know how much he loved her.

There were a couple of problems with that, of course. One was that she was now dating the captain of the eighth grade football team. Danny Brasco was a surly sort of guy who liked to display his bravado by beating up on kids half his size.

And Zachary was almost exactly half of Danny's size.

The other problem was that Zachary was quite comfortable around boys. But he was still painfully shy, and terribly awkward, when face to face with the fairer sex. He stammered and stuttered and looked like a fool.

So as much as he desperately wanted, or more accurately needed, to tell Amy how he felt, the situation grew more and more hopeless as each day went by.

Mr. Jenkins was trying to explain a basic algebraic equation on the board when the lights flickered twice, and then went out. Several of the students cheered and a couple of the boys high fived each other. Any distraction from the incessant droning of Mr. Jenkins was a welcome relief.

"All right, settle down. Everyone stay in their seats. You may talk quietly until we can resume. Anybody who leaves their seats will march right down to the office."

John Jay Middle School had been around since the 1950s, and was still equipped with old fashioned venetian blinds on its windows. Mr. Jenkins went over to the row of windows on the classroom's east wall and began rolling up each of the window blinds to let more light into the classroom.

At the third window, he peered out and said, "Well, that's odd."

Nothing will get the attention of a room full of teenagers faster than a teacher finding something odd. All of the boys, and several of the girls, stood up to look out the windows to see what Mr. Jenkins was talking about.

And the hair suddenly stood up on the back of Zachary's neck.

Outside the window, on Marbach Drive, was a long traffic jam of cars stopped suddenly in the tracks. Going absolutely nowhere. The wailing horns that would normally accompany such an event were eerily absent. For the horns didn't work without a car battery to power them. And all the car batteries had been suddenly and permanently shorted out.

One of the boys in the back of the class asked, "What the hell?" and everyone began murmuring, speculating on what was going on.

Zachary, of course, knew exactly what was going on. He pulled his cell phone out of his pocket. It was completely dead.

He whispered to his friend Paul, "Hey, check your phone. Is it working?"

"No. It's dead."

Another boy spoke up from the next row. "Mine too. That's weird."

Zachary knew what he had to do. He'd been drilled on it by his father many times. But first, he had a personal mission he had to accomplish.

He sat back down in his chair to catch his breath and to calm his nerves. He'd always been able to unstress by counting backwards from ten. In his mind he heard his own voice slowly counting, "Ten... nine... eight..."

When he got down to number one, he knew it was now or never.

He stood up with a resolve he'd seldom felt before.

He took two steps forward to where Amy was standing in front of her desk.

He said, "Amy..."

She turned, and Zachary wrapped his arms around her. He kissed her. Not a peck, either. He kissed her like the movie stars kissed in the movies.

Amy, caught totally off guard and not quite knowing what to do, did the only thing that came to her mind. She wrapped her arms around him and kissed him back.

It was a kiss of only a few seconds duration, but it was long enough to get his point across.

He broke free and took a step back. Somehow both of his hands found hers, and he looked into her deep brown eyes.

"Amy, I love you. I've always loved you. I just wanted you to know that."

Amy didn't say a word. She was still shocked by what happened, and didn't have a clue what to say.

But it didn't matter. No words were necessary on her part. Zachary did what needed to be done. He smiled at Amy and winked at her, then turned on his heels and walked out of the classroom.

Most of the girls stood watching with their mouths hanging open. One of the boys said, "Wait until Danny finds out."

Another said, "Zach will be dead meat then."

Mr. Jenkins called out, "Zachary, where are you going?"

He got no answer.

Zachary walked out of the class and into the semi-darkened hallway with the strangest smile on his face. And despite all the chaos that was going on outside the school at that moment, he was on cloud nine.

# -27-

"Ball! ball!"

Jordan was wide open. He'd lost his man and had a clear line to the basket. He looked up court and caught his buddy Jason's eye, and Jason let loose a long cross court pass aimed right for him.

The lights in the gym suddenly went out, half a second before the basketball hit Jordan squarely in the face.

"Dammit!"

He immediately tasted blood from a busted lip and felt the trickle of warm blood slowly rolling from his left nostril.

He went down to one knee.

The P.E. coach, Coach Garner, yelled, "Okay, nobody panic. Everybody just feel your way over to the door and we'll wait outside.

The P.E. gymnasium at Oliver Wendell Holmes High School was not attached to the school. It was an outbuilding separated from the school by the faculty parking lot. The gym had no windows, and it was pitch black inside.

Jordan pinched his tender nose and tilted his head back to stop the bleeding, all the while hoping it wasn't broken. He slowly made his way toward the exit, and when he was halfway there one of his classmates found it and propped it open. Sunlight came flooding in to mark the way to the outside world for the rest of the boys.

He was drenched in sweat. When Jordan played ball, he played for keeps. The breeze outside the gym felt good. His lip and nose were another matter completely.

Coach Garner came over and asked, "You okay, Harter? You need to go see the nurse for an ice pack?"

"No, sir. I'm okay."

Jordan and his friends chased each other through the parking lot, killing time while waiting for the lights to come back on in the gym.

They stopped as soon as the vice principal, Mr. Martin, came out of the admin building and headed for his car.

They watched as Mr. Martin tried using his keyless remote to unlock his car, and chuckled at the baffled look on his face when it wouldn't work.

They continued to watch while he manually unlocked the door and got inside the car. Twenty seconds later, he stepped back out of the car, raised the hood, and peered under it.

One of the boys behind Jordan muttered under his breath, "That's what you get for buying a piece of crap."

He'd never say that loud enough for Mr. Martin to hear it, of course. But in his mind, it strengthened his street cred and got some laughs from some of his buddies.

Perhaps it was because his attention was still focused on his sore nose and bloody lip. Jordan had just witnessed a blackout, and the vice principal's car breaking down.

But it still didn't click.

Then, out of the corner of his eye, Jordan saw something else.

At the entrance to the parking lot, a few minutes before, another teacher had been pulling in. His car had also stalled, fifty yards away, and he was also out of his car and looking under his hood.

The light finally came on in Jordan's head. He slipped away to the edge of the parking lot and climbed on the hood of a pickup truck. From his higher vantage point, he could see over a row of shrubbery and down to Ingram Street in front of the school.

To a sea of dead vehicles and frustrated drivers.

Jordan immediately turned and headed back into the gym.

It was still pitch black, of course. The sunlight only penetrated a few feet into the doorway. So very slowly, and very carefully so as not to hurt his already damaged face, he felt his way along the outer wall of the gym.

At one point he tripped over a pair of gym shoes someone had carelessly thrown up against the wall, but he didn't go down.

At the end of the west wall, he turned a corner and felt his way along the north wall of the gym twelve feet or so until he came to the doorway leading into the boys locker room.

Through the door he went into another sea of darkness. He knew that straight ahead there were five banks of lockers. He walked slowly though the blackness, both hands in front of him, until he felt the cold steel of the lockers.

From here he was home free. His was the second locker from the end and was easy to locate. He took the locker key hanging from a chain around his neck and used the fingers of both hands to insert the key into his padlock.

Once the lock was open he let it fall away to the floor. He knew he wouldn't be needing it again.

As he changed in the darkness, his mind raced a mile a minute. He knew he had to get out of here, and he knew how. What worried him was what his sudden departure would do to Sara. They hadn't been going together for long, but they'd hit it off great from the start. He really liked her, and she'd already confessed in a tender moment a few days before that she was falling in love with him.

There were two things that worried him. The first was that he still hadn't told her about the blackout, or his family's plan to disappear into the hill country when it happened.

The second thing that worried him was that Sara was a very sensitive girl. Not unlike a very delicate flower. She seemed somehow quite vulnerable, although she still hadn't explained to him exactly why.

It was because of that vulnerability that he worried what effect his sudden disappearance would have on her. Would she feel betrayed? Heartbroken? Abandoned?

He was suddenly very sad that he wasn't going to have a chance to tell her goodbye.

It took him a full twenty minutes to get dressed. When he was finally done, he turned slowly in the darkness and made his way back into the gymnasium.

This time traversing the gym was a piece of cake. With the double doors still propped open on the far side of the gym, he had a beacon of light to guide him, and nothing to block his way. He merely aimed himself at the light and jogged toward it.

A couple of his friends, sitting on the steps outside and still in their P.E. gear, were surprised to see Jordan coming quickly out the door in jeans and a t-shirt. As he jumped off the stoop, they shouted after him, "Hey, man! Where are you going?"

He ignored them and went on his way.

The student parking lot was on the opposite end of the main building. It was a relatively short walk though one of the main hallways, but when the hallways were black as the night, it would take too long to get through them. He figured it would be quicker to walk around the school.

And it was while walking around the school, past the orchestra hall, that he encountered Sara.

# -28-

Linda was in her car that Monday morning, going out to do a home visit on one of the clients for her home health company. She'd been in the Cruz home several times in the past, and had always walked away with a smile on her face.

They were a sweet old couple who'd been married for forty something years, and were still very much in love.

During her last home visit, Rosa Cruz asked Linda out of the blue if she liked to waltz.

Linda said she didn't know how.

Rosa said, "Oh, you should learn ballroom dancing. We were watching a television program last night, called 'Dancing with the Stars.' They were doing the waltz, and it brought back so many memories."

Her loving husband Charlie, as if on cue, got up from his easy chair and walked over to her. He held out his hand and said, "May I have this dance?"

Rosa blushed, as she probably did for their first dance fifty years before. And then she stood up and let him whirl her across the floor. Linda just stood back and watched. And smiled.

Somehow these two always managed to restore her faith in love and humanity.

She was looking forward to this morning's visit with Rosa and Charlie and had even stopped to buy Rosa a bouquet of flowers.

As Linda sat at a traffic light on Bitters Road, She saw what she would later describe to Joyce as a mirage-type wave in the distance.

"You know, like when you're driving through the desert, and way ahead on the road in front of you, the highway seems to get all wavy and blurred. It was kinda like that. All the buildings in the distance suddenly got blurry.

"Then the traffic lights went out, and my car died at the same time. It freaked me out, but just a bit. Then I looked around and realized that everybody else's cars had also died. The marquee at the movie theater there at the intersection, that had been advertising movies and show times just a few seconds before, was now black. That's when I *really* started to freak out."

Linda froze in her car seat, unsure of what to do. She stared straight ahead for a full two minutes, wondering if Scott's prediction was really coming true.

She had only half believed him about the blackout. She'd always known that he was a smart man, and not prone to wild conspiracy theories or outlandish tales. But at the same time, she didn't want the blackout to happen. And that part of her always hoped that he was just crazy, and that his prediction would never come true.

Finally, she knew she had to act. After trying her ignition key a couple of times, just to make sure, she stepped out of the car. She took her keys and her purse and carefully locked her car. Then she laughed at her own stupidity. It wasn't like anyone was going to get in it and drive away.

She went to her trunk and opened it with her key. Reaching into the back of the trunk, she dragged the backpack forward and opened it up. She took her pocketbook and a few essential items from her purse and threw them into the backpack. No sense carrying both for the long journey that was to come.

Scott had showed her how to assemble the bicycle in her trunk. He was patient with her, because he knew that she had no aptitude for anything mechanical.

"There are just three steps," he'd explained.

"Take the frame out first and put it upside down. I bought you one of the lightest frames on the market. It may look heavy, but you'll be amazed at how light it is.

"Put the back wheel on first. You can tell the back wheel because it's the one with the sprockets on it.

"Be sure you remember to wrap the chain around the smallest sprocket and then to slide the wheel all the way back in the channel. Then tighten the wing nuts as tight as you can get them.

"After the back wheel is on, put the front wheel on. Again, tighten the wing nuts as tightly as you can. Once the front wheel is on, you're ready to ride."

Scott had even had her assemble the bike three or four times in front of him, just to make sure she could do it. And when she assembled it without problems, he had her ride it around and helped her adjust the handlebars and seat.

With the memory of Scott's training as her guide, Linda was able to assemble the bike and ride away from her car within five minutes or so. A couple of people tried to flag her down to ask her for help. As Scott had instructed, she ignored them and rode right past.

"You don't know who may be a good person, and who may just push you aside and take your bike," he'd said. "And besides, there will be absolutely nothing you can do to help them. You cannot give them a ride. You cannot go to a telephone and call for help. You are no use to them at all. So just pass them by and get yourself to my house as quickly as you can."

Even with a bicycle to aid her in her journey, Linda was still almost twenty miles from Scott's house in north San Antonio. She would indeed get there as quickly as possible.

But it would still take awhile.

# -29-

Scott rolled over in bed and through groggy eyes wondered why it was so bright in the room. Then he noticed a note from Joyce on the pillow beside him.

He'd had a rough night's sleep, tossing and turning most of the night and trying to get comfortable. He'd strained his back the day before. Nothing serious, and he didn't even realize how he did it. All he knew was that even after six Tylenol, he was still looking at the ceiling at three in the morning wondering if he'd ever sleep again.

He'd obviously dozed off sometime after that, and had managed to sleep through his usual Monday morning routine of getting up, having breakfast with Joyce, Linda and the boys, and bidding them all goodbye as they left for the day.

He rubbed his eyes and read the note Joyce had left.

*Hi honey.*

*Decided you needed your rest more than breakfast so I turned off your alarm. Jordan is taking Zach to school. I expect a late day so I'll pick them up at your house and bring them home tonight. Expect us around seven. Let me know if you want me to stop and pick up dinner. Love you.*

Scott smiled and thought how lucky he was to have a woman in his life as thoughtful and sweet as Joyce. Then he rolled over and went back to sleep.

He never even noticed that his bedside clock, and everything else in the house, was no longer working.

# -30-

At John Jay Middle School, the halls were dark. Luckily, the doors at the end of each hallway were propped open during most of the school day unless the weather was bad. And today was a beautiful day.

Zachary stepped out of his algebra class after doing something he should have done years before but didn't have the guts. Now he felt accomplished and emboldened. He turned to his right and strode down the hallway with a purpose.

Luckily, his locker was close enough to the exit doors to be dimly lit. He only screwed up the combination once. He second time he slowed down a bit and nailed it.

He took the black backpack down from the hook where he dutifully hung it each day when he got to school. He never used it during the school day. He was smart enough to not need most of his textbooks, so unless he had a specific reading assignment in American Lit, he seldom took his books to class. This "doomsday bag," as he had come to call it, therefore sat on its hook from morning to afternoon, when he'd retrieve it just before getting on school bus 245 for the long ride home.

But not today. Today the doomsday bag was being liberated a little earlier than usual.

"Shouldn't you be in class?"

Zachary turned to see Coach Zarzamora.

There wasn't any love lost between the two. Coach Zarzamora was the man who terrorized Zachary on the track on a daily basis, belittling him for his lack of athletic skills and forcing him to run an endless number of laps.

"Nope. Not anymore."

Coach Zarzamora was not used to being sassed.

"Excuse me? What's that supposed to mean?"

Zachary put the black backpack on his back, slammed the locker shut, and turned to face the hated coach. And for the second time on this day, he found the inner strength and courage to do something he never would have thought of doing before.

He looked Coach Zarzamora in the eyes and said, "Figure it out yourself, dumbass."

Then he walked out the door and never looked back.

He walked across the school parking lot and was stopped by a desperate motorist.

"Excuse me," the man said. "I have to make a phone call. Which way is the office?"

"It's through that door over there. But none of the phones are working."

He saw the look of disappointment on the man's face and felt bad for him. But there was nothing he could do to help, and he had his own problems to deal with.

He tried his best to remember everything his father had told him.

"If the blackout happens while you're at school, you'll have to walk home. I know it's a long way. But trust me, son, you can do this. I have faith in you. You are strong in body and mind, and you can do it.

"The pack has bottles of water and granola bars. Do not take them out in public. People will be desperate to have them and might take them from you. If anybody asks what's in the backpack, tell them school books and keep walking.

"Walk down the freeway. It's the most direct route. It will look like a parking lot. All of the cars will be dead and abandoned.

"When you get thirsty or hungry, crawl inside one of the abandoned cars. Only then do I want you to take the water and granola bars out of the bag. Duck down in the seats as much as you can so people cannot see you have food and water. If they see you, they may try to take them from you. And they may be violent when they do.

"While you're ducking down in the seats, I want you to take the little metal box out of the backpack. Open it up and take out the walkie talkie. There's a card in there also. Read the instructions on the card and follow them to the letter."

To a good kid like Zachary, who was used to following all the rules, he felt like a fish out of water.

He actually felt guilty walking off campus in the middle of a school day, despite the circumstances. It just seemed to go against his grain, and he even turned around a couple of times to see if the school's truant officers were following him.

When he got to the street corner, he instinctively stopped and waited for the "walk" sign to illuminate. After a few seconds, he realized his folly and stepped out into a once bustling street that now more resembled a parking lot than a thoroughfare.

Everywhere he looked, people were rushing around, going in a dozen different directions. Many of the women were crying, and almost everyone had a look of panic on their faces.

It struck Zach as odd, that he alone among all these people, was calm and walking leisurely. Then it struck him that he was the only one among them who knew exactly what was going on. And more importantly, he was the only one who knew his destination. Everyone else was unsure where to go, what to do, how to protect themselves.

Only he, Zachary Harter, a fourteen year old average kid, had his act together this particular morning.

It gave him a sense of empowerment and a feeling of great strength.

And as he walked down the center of Interstate 35, though the heart of San Antonio, he was a boy without fear. At this moment, he felt like he was king of the world.

He had no idea what time it was. Joyce had given him an old fashioned watch months before. It had to be wound by hand every couple of days, but it kept good time.

Today, of all days, it was at home, sitting on the night table where he'd forgotten it.

He knew it was almost ten thirty when the power went out. Algebra was his last class before lunch, and he seldom got through the class without his stomach starting to growl.

And now, two hours into his walk, the adrenaline started to wear off and his legs started to tire, and he started to feel hunger pangs.

The feeling of invincibility was replaced by a feeling of fatigue, and a desire to sit down and have some food. There's a fine line between being a hero and wanting a hero sandwich, he decided.

He started looking for a vehicle that was unlocked and would offer him refuge.

The freeway was almost deserted now. Of people, at least. There were still cars pretty much everywhere, spaced four to six car lengths apart when their engines all sputtered and died.

Some were locked, some weren't.

He selected a Ford F-150 pickup. It was high off the ground, and he reasoned it would be harder for people to see him there.

The windows on this truck were very heavily tinted too, and that was a plus.

He crawled inside, depressed both door locks, and laid across the seat to rest.

# -31-

Joyce had her bike assembled in no time at all. Ten minutes after running from her office at a full sprint, she was on her bike, riding through residential streets, on her way to the Interstate 10 connector.

Several panicked people tried to flag her down to ask her for help. Or maybe their plans were more sinister. In any event, she ignored them and biked on past.

It wasn't that she didn't feel for them. They each had their own personal crisis they there dealing with. She knew that. But she couldn't waste time helping other people solve their problems when she had problems of her own.

She knew that Scott had no plans to get out today because of his back. That meant he was still at the compound, seventy miles from his house. And she knew that he'd have to drag one of the all wheel drive Gators out of the Foley barn and prep it before he could set out to meet up with them. And on a Gator, it would take awhile to get down that mountain.

So as much sympathy as she felt for the people around her, she would not, could not, stop to help them. She had her own problems to deal with. It was up to her and Linda to find and protect the boys until Scott arrived.

After she rounded the last corner before Interstate 10, Joyce came across a uniformed policeman standing in the road. Immediately upon seeing her approaching, he held up his hand for her to stop.

She sped up. He held out both hands and shouted, "Stop! Police!"

Joyce knew what he wanted. If she had stopped, he would have commandeered her bicycle. He'd have said it was emergency police business. And then she'd be afoot, and it would take her hours longer to get to her destination.

So Joyce did something she'd never have dreamed of doing under any other circumstances. She disobeyed an officer of the law and sped right past him. To hell with him. She had her own emergency. And hers was more important.

At least to her it was.

An hour into her ride, Joyce needed a break. She found that although riding a bicycle is something you never forget how to do, having the stamina and wind to ride it for long distances was something that got harder with age.

She remembered riding her bike in her youth, and how she could go for hours without being winded.

Obviously those days were gone forever. After an hour her legs ached and burned, and her lungs fought for every breath.

She was back off the highway now and on surface streets. She looked around her and didn't see anyone close enough to be a threat, so she stopped to catch her breath.

By car, she was only half an hour from Scott's house. By bicycle it was a different story completely.

She estimated that she was still a good three hours away now. And that's if she rode straight through. But the sun was high in the sky now, and she was very quickly becoming exhausted. As much as she hated to admit it, riding straight through probably wasn't going to happen.

Joyce looked at her watch for the tenth time. She was the one who had the forethought to go on the internet the previous spring and to purchase everyone windup watches.

Jordan thought she was joking. "How can a watch run without a battery?"

"Easy. It has a spring inside of it. You wind the spring and it runs for a couple of days. Then you wind it again. As long as you remember to wind it every couple of days it'll keep good time."

Jordan was still skeptical. But Joyce was able to find such watches on the internet, and let each of the boys choose the ones they wanted.

She paid a premium price for them, but they were accurate and not subject to damage from solar flares. Scott's lost about a minute a day, but Joyce joked that it didn't matter, because he was always behind everybody else anyway.

It was now almost twelve. She was adjacent to a large park, with a huge stand of trees. She figured this was as good a place as any to hide the bike, take a break, and try out her walkie talkie.

She took the small Foley box out of her backpack and opened it. She smiled when she saw that Scott had placed a small box of candy hearts in the box along with the walkie and two sets of batteries. Scott had a rough exterior, but he had a romantic side too. And he always knew just the thing to make her smile.

Even in the worst of circumstances.

"Scott, are you there?"

She knew he wouldn't be, unless he'd made an unscheduled trip into town for some reason. And she knew that was very unlikely, because he was a meticulous planner who seldom did anything on the spur of the moment.

No, it was much more likely that he was at that very moment on the Gator, making a bee-line to San Antonio to meet everyone at his house.

The trouble was, there was seventy miles between the two locations, and Gators didn't move very fast.

They had tested the radios when they first got them. Even though the owner's manual claimed an effective range of "up to twenty miles," that was under ideal conditions.

In reality, the "real world" range was more like twelve miles.

Joyce didn't expect to be able to raise Scott for at least a couple more hours. But she gave it a shot anyway.

She tried again.

"Scott, this is Joyce. Come in."

No answer. So she tried someone else.

"Linda, this is Joyce. Come in."

"This is Linda. Go ahead, Joyce."

At last. A friendly voice.

"Linda, where are you?"

"I'm sitting in a storm drain under Highway 281. Taking a break and getting a much needed drink. How about you?"

"I'm at a park about a third of the way between work and Scott's house. I'm not sure I'll make it there by nightfall, but I'm going to give it my best shot. Have you talked to the boys?"

"No, I've been trying every little while. They were instructed not to use their radios unless they were in a safe place. I hope they call soon."

The radio began to crackle, and a new voice came on.

"Mom, it's me, Zach."

"Zachary! My baby! Are you okay?"

"Yes. I'm fine. But my legs aren't used to walking this much."

"Where are you, honey?"

"I'm sitting in a big pickup on Loop 410. I don't know where exactly, I forgot the name of the last exit. I'm eating my lunch, and I just now turned on the radio and you guys were there."

"So you haven't heard from Jordan either?"

"No, ma'am."

"Zachary, you've got to be strong and brave, okay?"

"Sure, Mom. I'm not a little kid anymore."

"I know that, honey. But I also know you're tired, and it is important that you make it to the house before dark. You are the closest one to the house right now. And even though you don't have a bicycle, you should still beat everybody else. You just have to be tough and push yourself. Okay?"

Linda couldn't see him roll his eyes.

"Okay, Mom. I'll be fine. Have you heard from Dad?"

"Not yet, honey. But he has a long way to come before he'll be within radio range. Honey, do you remember what to do when you get to the house."

"Yes, ma'am."

He knew the drill. They had talked about it a hundred times before.

"I go into Dad's office and look in the drawer where he keeps his files. In the very back there's a red folder with my name on it. Inside the folder are very specific instructions on what to do while I'm waiting on everybody else. I really hate pop quizzes, Mom. How did I do?"

Linda laughed.

"You did great, honey."

"Can I ask you something?"

"Sure, honey. What's on your mind?"

"While I was walking, I was thinking about some of my friends. In school and on the block. What do you think will happen to them after we're gone?"

She swallowed hard.

"Well, honey, I just don't know. I mean, I know they will survive. But they will have it a lot harder than we will because they haven't prepared the way we have."

"But they won't die or anything?"

"No, sir. They won't die just because the power went out."

"Okay. Thank you, Mom. I love you."

"I love you too, son. Now finish eating and get back on your way, okay?"

"Okay. Bye."

She didn't have to worry about this little trooper. He was holding up well.

The three got off their radios and got back on the road.

# -32-

Scott was scrambling. Thanks to his laziness, he was already an hour behind schedule, and he was cursing himself every step of the way.

Once he rolled out of bed and discovered the power was off, he checked his phone. It was dead. He picked up the flashlight on his night table. Dead.

He fairly flew out to the Ford Explorer parked out in front of the house. Then the F-150 pickup. They were both deader than doornails.

The old professor was right. It had really happened. And none of their lives would ever be the same again.

He went outside to the Butler building he'd modified into a Foley cage. First, he swung open the double doors. In front of him was a huge plywood box covered on all sides by heavy wire mesh.

The mesh on each side of the box was connected with wire ties to allow a steady current of electricity around the box when the EMP hit. He had to snip the wire ties connecting the front of the box with the top and sides before he could open the box.

Once that was done, it was simply a matter of easing the heavy door, which was hinged on the bottom, down to the ground. The door was heavily reinforced to take several hundred pounds of weight, since it acted as a vehicle ramp in addition to a door.

Scott scrambled into the box and jumped on his Gator. He pulled the choke halfway out and held his breath.

It fired right up. The Foley cage had worked as advertised.

He quickly inventoried the supplies that had already been loaded onto the tiny pickup bed on the back of the Gator. A case of bottled water. A large box of trail mix. A pair of battery operated night vision goggles, and extra batteries. Two two-way radios with batteries. An assault rifle and a 9 mm Glock, with ammunition. A five gallon fuel can, full of fuel to augment the already full tank. Tents, blankets and sleeping bags.

He had everything he needed. He drove the Gator outside the compound and locked everything up. Then he drove down the long and winding drive to the narrow road that fronted the property. He turned right and drove a short distance to the string of high tension power lines he'd follow to his house in the city.

But before he began his journey, he had one more thing to do.

He got off the Gator and took a spool of brown thread. When placed close to the ground, it would be practically invisible.

Scott ran a piece of the thread completely across the roadway, and about six inches above it. He secured it by tying each end to a rock.

Then, in a flash, he was back on the Gator and on the road.

There were two gravel roads that the power company had used to maintain the towers. One ran along the west side of the towers, and about twenty feet away from them. The second was between the legs of the two hundred foot tall towers. That's the one Scott chose.

His logic was sound. If someone saw him coming from afar and got the hare brained idea to try to knock him off the Gator, it wouldn't work. It was a fifty yard sprint from the brush to the road beneath the towers. Scott would see them in time to take evasive action.

And if they just wanted to shoot him off the Gator, they'd have to be a good shot. Hitting a fast moving target from fifty yards away wasn't easy, unless you were an experienced hunter. And at the first sign of trouble, Scott would crouch down to make the shot even harder.

He expected to make good time, helped by the fact that the utility company did an excellent job of keeping their service roads maintained. Although made of gravel, it was very tightly packed and smooth. There were no potholes at all.

In addition, the compound was over six hundred feet higher in elevation than his home in San Antonio. It was all gradual, of course, and barely noticeable over the seventy mile stretch. But it meant there were no uphill grades to slow down his progress.

He looked at his watch, and then the sun in the sky. Then he did some math in his head and figured that, barring any trouble, he'd make it to his house and meet up with everyone else around ten p.m.

He just hoped that everyone else was there when he arrived.

# -33-

"Jordan, where are you going?"

His girlfriend Sara had been sitting in the orchestra room, her violin in her lap, looking out the window. Waiting for the power to come back on so they could finish the chair competition they'd been working on.

Suddenly, out of the far parking lot, she saw Jordan, walking quickly like a man on a mission.

The orchestra room had a door that opened to the parking lot, to make it easy for a truck to pick up their instruments for concerts at other schools. Sara took advantage of that fact and quietly slipped out the door to flag Jordan down.

Mr. Rodriguez, the orchestra director, didn't care. He was sound asleep at his desk in the back of the classroom.

Jordan was somewhat taken aback by Sara's sudden appearance.

"Baby, get back in the school. You shouldn't be out here."

"You're out here. Why can't I be?"

She had a point.

"And where are you going?"

Jordan was between a rock and a hard place, and he knew it.

Keeping the whole compound thing a secret from Sara was one thing. Outright lying to her was something else entirely.

"Look. You're not supposed to know this. The lights are off for good. They're never coming on again. None of the vehicles will ever run again. The world has gone back to the stone age, and it'll be that way for the rest of our lives."

Sara's jaw dropped.

"Jordan, what on earth are you talking about?"

"Sara, my dad found some professor's notes. He predicted this. And my dad believed him, and we've been planning for this for over a year now. Since long before we met."

"Why didn't you tell me?"

Jordan was at a loss. He knew there were no words that would justify his behavior.

"Where are you going? What are you going to do?"

"I'm going up into the mountains. My family built a safe place to live. Someplace where we'll still have electricity, and be able to grow our own food. I'm sorry."

Sara pondered his words. Then tears welled up in her eyes and she looked at him.

Her words were but a whisper.

"But what about me? Where will I go?"

"You'll wait here with everybody else until your parents come for you. They'll protect you and care for you."

She flew into a panic.

"From St. Louis?"

Jordan's heart hit the floor. He'd forgotten that Sara's parents were out of town. They'd gone to Missouri to attend some great aunt's funeral. Sara was all alone.

Sometimes, when under pressure and faced with an important decision, we have a tendency to do something really stupid.

But sometimes, under the very same circumstances, we do something very noble.

Jordan hesitated for only a moment. Then he took her hand and started through the parking lot with her.

"You're coming with me."

Sara left everything behind: her violin, her books, her purse. But it didn't matter. She had Jordan, and she was trusting him to guide her. If he was right, their lives would never be the same again. If he was right, they had only each other. From now on.

They went to his car, and they made plans on the fly as he assembled the bicycle.

"Your house is only a few blocks out of the way. We'll go by there first. You can pack a bag with a few clothes. You won't need many. I think you're the same size as my mom. While we're there you can write a note to your mom and dad. You can tell them you're safe, and you're with my family. And that we'll bring you home when it's safe to do so."

He got the bike put together and tied the backpack behind the bike seat.

"Get on," he said. "But don't go too fast. I'm not a fast runner."

They made it a couple of miles before they had to stop and rest. Sara stepped off the bike and walked it alongside Jordan as he caught his breath. A couple of men eyed them from fifty yards away, and Jordan became worried.

"If they come over this way, it's probably to steal the bike. If they start to approach us, I want you to jump on it and ride as fast as you can. Don't stop until you get to your house. I'll meet you there."

But the men seemed to lose interest and walked in another direction. Perhaps they saw the look on Jordan's face and thought they could find an easier target.

Or perhaps they never had any ill intent and Jordan was just paranoid.

They made it to Sara's house within an hour and a half. Jordan was exhausted.

Sara unlocked the house and they rolled the bike into the living room with them.

Jordan collapsed on the couch.

"I'm beat. Grab just what you need. Remember whatever you bring, we'll have to lug all the way to my house. And don't forget to write your parents a note."

After ten minutes, Jordan went to the refrigerator and guzzled a full bottle of water. He knew it would probably cause his stomach to cramp during the run to his house. But it tasted so good he just couldn't find the will power to stop drinking.

Sara came out of her bedroom with a bright pink "Hello Kitty" backpack.

"Great," he muttered. "How old are you again?"

"Oh, shut up. My regular backpack is in my locker at school. This is an old one."

He couldn't help but smile. Sara was becoming a woman. But she still had a lot of little girl in her.

"Did you write a letter for your folks?"

Sara held up a sealed envelope with "Mom and Dad" scrawled across the front.

She laid it on the kitchen counter and took a second bottle of water from Jordan.

She drank half the bottle, unzipped "Hello Kitty," and dropped the half filled bottle into the bag. Then she put the bag on her back, tightened the straps, and said, "I'm ready to go."

They walked out the door and locked it behind them.

Sara had only a few secrets in her life, and only one that she kept from Jordan. That was, of course, until now.

Now she kept two from him. For she knew something that he didn't. She knew that the envelope she placed on the kitchen counter held no note. It was completely empty.

# -34-

Zachary was exhausted. His feet hurt, his back ached, and he just wanted to lie down and crash for a couple of hours.

But he knew there was way too much to be done.

As expected, he was the first one to the house. Although he was the only one on foot, he had by far the shortest distance to travel. And he had the energy of youth. Everybody else was old. Well, except his brother. But Jordan had a very long way to ride his bike.

He suddenly got an image of his mom riding a bicycle. For some reason, it struck him as funny and he chuckled as he went to the kitchen and took a bottle of water out of the refrigerator.

For a brief instant he wondered to himself why it wasn't very cold. Then he remembered the situation they were in, and he felt very stupid. Good thing there was no one else around and he didn't make the observation out loud. He'd have felt like a dumbass.

He went into his Dad's office and found the folder with his name on it. He opened it up to find three pages of instructions from his father:

*Dear Zach,*

*If you're reading this note, it means that the EMP has hit the earth and that the power is out for good. It also means that you're the first one home.*

*It's probably getting pretty close to dark. There are some things you'll need to do before the sun goes down. The first thing is, lock the front door again. Do not leave it unlocked for your mom and brother and Joyce. They have their own keys and can get in. If you don't lock it, looters may come in and could hurt you.*

*If you haven't already done that, do it now. Then come back and we'll continue.*

*Now turn your walkie talkie back on. You can leave it on now, unless you hear someone breaking in. Then turn it off immediately and hide.*

*Having your walkie talkie on constantly should help calm your nerves, and will make it easier to find out where everyone else is.*

*I will probably be too far away to reach when you get this. But you can try everyone else. Remember not to panic, though, if they do not answer. It doesn't mean anything has happened to them. It only means that they are out in the open where other people can see them.*

*The next thing I want you to do is open my bottom right dresser drawer. You'll find a larger version of the Foley box that was in your back pack.*

*Open it up and you'll find six miner's lights and several packages of AA batteries.*

*Put the batteries in all of the lights. Put one around your neck and give the others to your mom and Jordan and Joyce as they arrive. That will make it easier for everyone to see once the sun goes down. When it gets dark, just put the light on your forehead, tighten the strap and turn it on. The light will shine at whatever you're looking at.*

*Okay, good. You're doing fine.*

*Now go to the kitchen and pull out a stack of dinner plates from the cupboard. The white ones with the blue trim. They are light and shatterproof.*

*I know this will seem dumb to you, but do it anyway. Take the dinner plates and place one on the floor in the center of each room. Then come back here.*

*Now go to the bottom left drawer of my dresser and open it. You'll find twelve large room candles. They're kind of heavy, so you can probably only carry two or three at a time. Go put one candle on each dinner plate. Each candle has three wicks, and will light up each room after dark.*

*There are three lighters in the same drawer. Put one in your pocket and the other two on the kitchen counter.*

*Now go around the house and close all of the blinds and draperies. It will make it dark in the house, but you'll have your miner's light so you'll be okay.*

*The last thing I want you to do is go to my bedroom and watch out the window. You'll have a clear view of the whole street.*

*Just stay there and watch. When you see Joyce or your mom or your brother arrive, meet them downstairs and give them a miner's light. Then go back to the window and watch again.*

*PAY ATTENTION TO THIS ONE. IT'S VERY IMPORTANT... If you see someone approaching that you don't know, and if they break into the house, crawl under my bed and stay there quietly until they leave. Don't try to confront them or fight them. You might get hurt. Just let them take whatever they want and leave.*

*Also, if you hear someone breaking in the back door or breaking a window, do the same thing. I don't think the looters will come out until well after dark. I also don't think they will try to break in the back. Duke will bark and probably chase them away, unless they are bold enough to shoot him. I don't think they'll do that. I think they'll just go elsewhere. But remember, expect the unexpected. Just in case.*

*Remember that I love you, son. I'll be there as quickly as I can.*

*-Dad-*

Zachary knew his father had planned this for a very long time and trusted his judgment. Even though he thought it very strange to put each candle on top of a white dinner plate, he followed instructions to the letter.

It took him almost an hour to get everything finished. When he finally looked out the window, he could tell from the position of the sun that it would be getting dark soon.

For the first time since the ordeal began he felt lonely and sad. Maybe it was because this was the first time since the ordeal began when he had absolutely nothing to do.

Except wait.

Then, suddenly, it dawned on him. He'd been so busy doing the things on his list, he'd never turned on his walkie talkie.

He ran downstairs from his father's room and grabbed the small radio from his back pack. He put the extra set of batteries into the front pocket of his jeans and walked back up the stairs, turning the radio on as he went.

He looked through the curtains of his dad's bedroom window and saw a couple of kids playing in their yard three doors down. Four of the moms had gathered in one of their front yards a little farther than that.

There was no other activity.

He keyed the microphone.

"Dad, this is Zach. Come in."

No answer.

"Mom, this is Zach. Come in."

No answer.

"Joyce, this is Zach. Come in."

Despite his dad's pleas not to panic, he started to feel a little anxiety.

Then his walkie crackled to life.

"This is Joyce. Where are you, sweetie?"

"I'm at home. Watching the street from Dad's window. Where are you?"

"I'm close. I'm taking my final break, and then I've got about a mile to go. I'll be there in about twenty minutes."

Zachary finally breathed a sigh of relief.

"10-4."

# -35-

Joe saw Linda coming from a great distance away. Long before she saw him.

And normally Joe Warner wasn't a bad man.

But these were desperate times. And in desperate times a man, any man, will often do things he ordinarily wouldn't.

Joe was tired of walking. And it would be dark soon.

He'd spent a lot of years in the Navy. Hadn't really done much of note. Mostly rode a desk and did just what he had to do to get his paycheck. But he did go to sea a couple of times when he ran out of ways to dodge it. And one of the things he remembered from his Navy days was how to read the sun.

As long as he knew what day of the month it was, he could estimate the setting of the sun within three or four minutes, three or four hours in advance.

And his training taught him, within three or four minutes, that he had an hour and ten minutes left before the sun disappeared beneath the horizon.

Something else his Navy days had taught him was that he wasn't much of a man. Not, at least, when it came to defending himself in hand to hand combat. He was a mousy kind of guy, whose mouth always got him into trouble, and who got challenged to fights on a regular basis.

He ran when he could. And when he couldn't run, he got pummeled.

The memories still stung. But they also made him very aware that he was a coward and a weakling. And that he would not survive well in a hostile environment of any type.

The sixty extra pounds he'd packed on since the Navy didn't help his situation any either. He was desperate to get home, so he could barricade himself in his house and pull out his weapons for self preservation.

But he knew he couldn't make it before it got dark, and that terrified him.

Yes, in the bleakest of circumstances, desperate men will do desperate things.

And there was a woman, alone on a bicycle, a block and a half away.

And she was coming right at him.

Linda was making good time. She was less than an hour away now. She was off the freeway, and it should be smooth sailing from here.

She was surprised. She was expecting it to be much more chaotic than it was.

Perhaps it hadn't sunk in yet that this was more than just an occasional power outage. Perhaps people were waiting for the power company to get everything turned back on again. They'd still be without cars and cell phone service. But at least they'd be able to have lights in their houses. They could cook their dinners and turn on their televisions to the evening news. Maybe there they could find out why all the cars stopped working. And more importantly, when they would start back up again.

She'd seen a few looters breaking into a darkened convenience store, and two teenaged boys smashing car windows and then rooting through the cars. But most of the people she saw looked relatively calm.

But then again, she had yet to encounter Joe Warner.

Joe was crouched behind a Ford Expedition, waiting for just the right moment to pounce. He'd already taken his 9 mm Colt from the holster on the back of his waistband. It was legal. He had a concealed carry license and all. He never expected to use it in a situation like this. But he would do whatever he needed to do to get home to a safe environment.

And he was running out of daylight.

When Linda was almost parallel to the Expedition's back bumper, Joe Warner pounced. Instantly, he was on the roadway in front of her, in a shooter's stance, both hands on the butt of the weapon and his finger on the trigger. One nervous twitch, and Linda would be dead.

"Stop right there!"

She did.

"What do you want?"

Even with the gun, he was more frightened than she was. She could see his hands shaking.

"Take it easy, Mister. I am no threat to you. Don't do anything that's going to ruin both of our lives."

"Get off the bike."

She did as she was told. With another assailant she might have argued the point, tried to talk him out of taking away her transportation.

But she could see that he was unstable. Dangerously so.

She popped the kickstand and stood the bike up. Then she held both hands out to her side and backed away from it.

"Take it, Mister. I'm tired of riding anyway. It's all yours."

She continued walking in the direction she'd been headed, backwards, so she could keep a close eye on this crazy man. She watched him get on her bicycle and very clumsily ride off in the direction she'd come. It was obvious he hadn't ridden a bike in many years. He wobbled and swayed and almost hit a couple of stalled cars before he finally got the hang of it.

It didn't help that still clutched in his right hand was his 9mm pistol. He dared not holster it until he was far away from Linda, for fear the petite woman who was one third his size would pounce on him and beat him to a pulp.

When Joe Warner was almost out of sight, Linda turned away from him and resumed her walk. Losing the bike would set her back, but she'd still be at the house before dark.

Ten minutes later she heard a flurry of gunshots in the direction Joe Warner had ridden.

They were a bit unnerving. But they were too far away from her to cause her any real concern. So she didn't put much thought into them.

She would never know that Joe Warner lay mortally wounded in the middle of the street two miles back.

She would never know that the teenaged boys she'd seen breaking into cars had noticed her riding past.

And that they laid in wait for her, thinking there was an even chance that she'd soon be returning from whatever trip she was taking.

The boys' weapons weren't legal like Joe's was, of course. Texas was a big second amendment state. Texas loves its guns, and even crazy schizophrenics like Joe Warner were able to easily obtain one. Or a hundred, if he wanted to.

If it were up to the Texas legislature, they'd have issued a gun permit to everyone upon birth. But they weren't quite there yet.

So it was still impossible for fifteen year old thugs to walk into a gun shop and buy a gun legally. These boys' guns came from burglaries.

But that didn't matter. Wherever they came from, they still worked, and were just as lethal as Joe Warner's.

They hadn't given Joe the same option he'd given Linda, to walk away and stay alive.

Joe, in fact, had never seen them. They'd hidden behind a parked car, just like he had, until he'd ridden past. Then they shot him four times in the back.

Joe Warner drifted off to eternal sleep wondering what hit him. But he'd never know.

## -36-

Misty Plain Drive was on an eight degree grade. Skateboarders loved it. School kids walking home from school each day, didn't. Especially when they were loaded down with school books or band instruments.

Door to door salesmen seldom came on Misty Plain Drive. It just wasn't worth the effort. Residents were even insulated to a large degree from Jehovah's witnesses, who tended to go elsewhere to talk to people about Jesus.

And so it was that the last quarter mile of Joyce's journey was also the worst. She was already exhausted by the time she got to the end of the street, and just didn't have the energy to put forth the extra leg muscle it took to get up that hill.

Zachary watched from the window in his Dad's bedroom as Joyce finally got off the bike and walked it the last hundred yards. Under other circumstances, he'd have thought of some smart aleck remark to say to her about it. Something about old women's bodies not being up to the task.

But these weren't ordinary circumstances. He'd cut her some slack today and let this one pass.

Instead, he met her at the front door, stood to one side as she wheeled the bicycle into the house, then gave her a really big hug.

For Joyce, it was exactly what she needed.

Zachary relocked the front door and quickly filled Joyce in on what he had done. Then, as his father had instructed, he headed back up the stairs to continue his watch.

Joyce stopped him halfway up the stairs.

"Zachary?"

He turned to look at her.

"Great job! I'm very proud of you."

He smiled. Then he turned and headed back up. It was nice to be appreciated. And yes, he was kinda proud of himself too.

Joyce got a bottle of water from the refrigerator and was happy to see it was still cool. As long as they kept the refrigerator door closed as much as possible, the food inside would stay fresh until they were long gone. Then the scavengers could help themselves to whatever was left.

She downed the water, almost in one gulp. She wasn't in bad shape for a woman her age. But she wasn't in such good shape that the bike ride she'd just finished was a piece of cake, either. It had kicked her ass. Especially the last couple of miles. And the incline up Misty Plain Drive, that final kick in the teeth, was like pouring salt in a wound. She hoped Linda and Jordan didn't struggle as much as she had.

She tried the radio to see if anyone else was on.

"Scott, this is Joyce. Are you on?"

Nothing.

"Linda? Jordan?"

Nothing for a few seconds. Joyce was getting ready to turn the radio back off when it sprang to life.

"Joyce, this is Linda."

"Linda, where are you?"

"I'm sitting in a deserted car a couple of miles from the house. My bike was stolen. I'm okay, though. I should be there about nine o'clock or so. Are you at the house yet?"

"Yes. I just got here. Zach is here too. You should be very proud of him, Linda. He followed his instructions to the letter. He's turning into a fine young man."

Zach was listening in from Scott's bedroom and couldn't help but break in.

"Hi, Mom. Are you sure you're okay?"

"Yes, honey, I'm fine. And good job! I'm so proud of you!"

He grinned from ear to ear.

Joyce got back on.

"Linda, have you heard from the other guys?"

"No, I'm afraid not. I've been trying off and on to get hold of Jordan, but he's been off the air for awhile now. I hope he's okay. I think Scott is probably still out of range."

"Yes, I agree. I'm going to leave my radio on all the time now that I'm at the house. When they call in, are there any messages you want me to pass on?"

"Just tell them to be careful and give them my love. I'm heading back out in a minute, and I'll see you soon."

"Okay, be safe."

## -37-

Joyce was certain that Scott was feverishly working his way off the mountain to them. She wasn't worried about him. Jordan, on the other hand, weighed heavily on her mind. They had grown quite close during the previous months. And although he wasn't her son, she pretty much considered him so.

She went to the kitchen and opened the refrigerator just long enough to remove a few things. A package of bologna. A jar of mayonnaise, another of mustard. A head of lettuce and a couple tomatoes. She laid everything on the counter and closed the door quickly, to keep most of the cold air inside, and spent the next ten minutes making a dozen sandwiches. She wrapped each of them in plastic zip-lock bags and returned everything but two of the bagged sandwiches to the refrigerator.

Then, on a lark, she opened the door one last time and took out a third sandwich, and two cans of Coca Cola.

At the top of the stairs, she called out to Zachary.

"Are you hungry, sweetie?"

"I'm starving."

She handed him two of the sandwiches and a soda and said, "Sit on the bed and take a break. I'll stand at the window and watch."

Between mouthfuls he asked, "Joyce… are you scared?"

"Of what, honey?"

"Oh, I don't know. Of all the violence that's going to take place, I guess."

"Well, not really. I mean, I suspect that most of the bad people out there think this is something going on with the power company. Most people probably think the lights are going to come back on any time, like they've always done before. I think that possibility will keep most of the bad guys off the streets tonight. There will probably be some looting, but I think they'll hit the stores, not the homes. I mean, the stores can't shoot at them, but homeowners can. I don't think it'll get dangerous in the neighborhoods for at least a few nights. And we'll be long gone by then."

"I'm worried about my friends."

"Oh, I know, honey. I'm not going to try to make light of the situation. It won't be easy on them. They'll have a much harder time of it than we will. But they've all got parents and other loved ones who will help them get through it."

"Is it true that people will have to grow everything they eat from now on?"

"Well, not right away, but eventually. I mean, there's a lot of food out there now, in people's cupboards, and in the supermarkets. No one is going to starve right away. But there's no way to make more of the kinds of foods you find at the supermarkets. Or a way to get it there. So after a few days or weeks, it will start to run low. And then people will have to start making some pretty tough choices. Either to steal it, or to find a way to make their own."

The radios squawked once more.

"Dad, Mom, Joyce, Gooberhead. This is Jordan. Is anybody out there?"

"Go ahead, Jordan."

"Joyce, is everybody okay?"

"Yes, dear. Are you getting close?"

"Yes, ma'am. I can't talk long, I see someone coming up ahead. We had to take a detour, I'll explain later. We should be there in an hour or so. Gotta go. I'll call again when I can."

Joyce looked at Zachary. They had the same thought, but only Joyce voiced the words.

"Did he just say 'we?'"

Zach shrugged his shoulders and said "Yep. Twice."

He finished his second sandwich and asked, "Want me to take watch again?"

"Yes, please. It's starting to get dark, and I need to get the candles lit."

She left Zach in the upstairs bedroom and made her way back to the kitchen, where she collected a lighter and made her way around the house, lighting the candles that Zachary had put out earlier. She saved Scott's bedroom for last, and told Zach, "I'm going to leave this room dark for now, sweetie. That way people on the outside can't see you from the street when you look out the window. Is that okay with you?"

"Sure, no problem. Joyce, what do you think Jordan meant when he said 'we?'"

"I don't know, honey. Maybe he has a mouse in his pocket?"

Zachary found this incredibly funny and laughed. It was the first good laugh he'd had all day.

Joyce asked, "Is your radio on?"

"Yes."

"Good. I'm going downstairs to prepare the weapons and start making preparations to evacuate. Call me if you see anyone coming near the house. And for sure call me when you see your mom or brother approaching, so I can let them in."

"Yes, ma'am."

Then he smiled and said, "But be sure you tell Jordan he has to leave his mouse outside."

At that moment, Duke began to bark in the back yard.

Joyce said, "You stay here. I'll check it out."

She walked across the hallway to the bedroom at the back of the house.

Blowing out the candle in the center of the room, she proceeded to the window and pulled the drapes to one side. Then she raised up the corner of one of the blinds and peeked into the back yard.

Duke, a four year old black lab, was barking at the neighbor's cat, who was perched atop the fence mocking him.

She reclosed the draperies, relit the candle, and eased back to Scott's room.

"He's just barking at the cat next door. It's nothing to worry about. I hope they go at it for awhile. His barking will scare off anybody we don't want back there."

"There's somebody coming up the street."

Joyce stood behind him and looked over his shoulder. It was a man she'd never seen before.

"Do you recognize him?"

"It might be Mr. Garcia. He walks kinda the same way. Kinda hard to tell without any streetlights."

In the moonlight, Joyce could make out something in the man's hand. She couldn't tell what it was, though. It wasn't long, like a rifle. It was more square, like a...

Zach beat her to the punch.

He said, "He's carrying a briefcase."

They watched as Mr. Garcia, an insurance salesman, walked up to the front door of his house across the street. For him it was the end of a long walk, from his car that had died several hours before and several miles away. They watched as his wife opened the door and hugged him, a lit candle in her hand. Then they disappeared inside their darkened house and closed the door.

# -38-

Joyce went downstairs to Scott's office. She went into his closet and moved several boxes out of the way, until she came to a long gun case hidden behind them.

The combination was Scott's birthday, 1227.

She opened the case and removed five weapons that were nesting on the soft gray eggshell foam inside. Two AR-15 rifles, and three Glock 9mm handguns. She put all the weapons aside, closed the case, and returned it to the corner of the closet.

The ammunition was stored separately, but she knew where it was too.

She walked up the stairs to Scott's dresser and pulled the bottom left drawer completely out. Months before, Scott had removed the locking mechanism that prevented it from being pulled too far out. It was the only drawer in the dresser that could be completely removed.

Joyce set the drawer off to one side. Then she reached inside the void the drawer had left, and felt the carpeted floor beneath the dresser. And on the left side of the space, up against the inside end panel of the dresser, she felt the magazines. Two each for the AR-15s, two each for the pistols. She pulled them out and set them aside. Then she returned the drawer to its original location.

She carried the magazines back to Scott's office and loaded the weapons. She didn't chamber any rounds, though, or take them off safe. She'd wait until there was a bigger threat. And she hoped it wouldn't be necessary, that they would make it back to their mountain hideaway without being challenged.

Once done, she went into the same file drawer that Zachary had pulled his folder from earlier.

She smiled when she noted that he'd left the drawer wide open. Zachary had a thing with open drawers. And leaving the toilet seat up. Jordan was the same way. Must be a teenage boy thing.

The light from the candles was no longer sufficient. Joyce reached up and turned on the small miner's light on her forehead, then looked through the folders at the back of the drawer. She found one that was bright yellow, her favorite color. It was marked with her name and a little heart.

She opened the folder and removed a single sheet of paper, written in Scott's handwriting.

*Dear Joyce,*

*If you're reading this, the solar storm has happened, and the EMP has come. I know this is a stressful time for you. I need for you to be strong. The boys will take their cue from you. If you don't panic, they won't either.*

*I don't know where I will be when the power goes out. All I can tell you is that I will be there as quickly as I can. However, if I am not there within twenty four hours, then something has happened to me. If that is the case, then I want you to do the following:*

*Go into the back yard, to the wooden storage building. Open the front doors, and you'll see what appears to be a large metal cage with plywood behind it.*

*It is the front door to a very large Foley cage, and the door is hinged at the bottom. When it is opened, the front will drop down to make a ramp for the two all wheel drive Gators on the inside.*

*On the side of the storage building is a wooden ladder. Take it to the front of the Foley cage with a knife.*

*Climb up the ladder and you'll find that the top of the door is tied to the metal at the roof by four plastic electrical ties. Snip those ties. Then move the ladder out of the way and you can lower the door. Please be careful. I installed two restrainers to keep it from opening too quickly, but it can still hurt you if you don't get out of its way.*

*The Gators are ready to go. I've checked them out every four or five days for over a year, and they're in good working order. Start them up and drive them into the yard.*

*In the beds of the Gators you'll find several things. Each one will have two five gallon containers of diesel. You'll need the extra fuel to make it back to the compound.*

*Also in the beds you'll find a box of AA batteries and five sets of night vision goggles. You'll need them because I want you to drive at night. There are also sleeping bags and tents in case you don't make it the first night. Once you get away from the city the area is heavily wooded. You can get away from the power lines and disappear into the woods, where you can safely camp during the day and wait for the darkness to return.*

*Follow the power lines that run behind the house. There is a road that runs through the center of each tower. Just stay on that road and head north.*

*The towers are numbered on the left side with reflective tape. With the night vision goggles on, the numbers are easy to see. After you pass tower number 20050, the next dirt road on the left will connect with the access road to the compound.*

*This part is important, honey... If I didn't show up, there was a good reason. It probably means somebody took me out. If I'm not there, you have to be extra cautious. I know you can shoot, and so can Linda. Be on your toes and watch out for other people. Assume anyone you encounter is a bad guy. Don't hesitate to shoot to defend yourself.*

*As for the Gators, they creep very well. If you put them in drive and let them crawl, they are almost silent. It is slow going, but is much safer. That is probably the safest way to get you there.*

*I hope it's a moot point. I hope to be there helping you and that we all come back together. But if I don't make it, I have faith in you, honey. You can do this. I know you can.*

*Good luck. I love you.*
*-Scott-*

Joyce wiped a tear from the corner of her eye. She could do this without Scott, sure. But she didn't want to. She'd developed quite a love for this man over the last few months. Losing him now was not an option she wanted to consider.

She put the note aside when she heard Zachary yell, "Joyce, it's Mom!"

Joyce rushed to the foot of the stairs and answered, "Okay, honey. Yell when she's in the yard and I'll open the door to let her in."

Linda, trudging up the hill toward the house, was exhausted. It was the most taxing thing she'd done physically in twenty years. Every bone in her body hurt. The last mile had seemed like ten, and under her breath she cursed the developer who decided to build this set of houses on a long uphill street.

As she neared the house, she put her radio up to her mouth to announce her arrival, but it was a wasted gesture. As if on cue, the front door opened. She practically fell into the comforting arms of Joyce.

"Boy, am I happy to see you."

Joyce helped Linda to the dining room table and brought her a sandwich and bottle of water.

"You and I can talk in a bit," she said. "Right now I'm going to go relieve Zach so he can come down and keep you company while you eat. I know he's been missing you a lot."

## -39-

After Linda ate and rested, she and Zachary joined Joyce in Scott's bedroom. The three shared idle talk and discussed things they needed to do in the coming hours.

Zachary uttered the question, "I wonder when Dad is going to call."

His words must have held magic. Mere seconds later, their radios sprang to life once again.

"Can anyone hear me? This is Scott."

The signal was weak and full of static, but his words were clear.

Joyce looked at Linda, who smiled and nodded her head in Zachary's direction.

Joyce said, "Go ahead and answer, Zach."

"Dad, this is Zach. Are you okay?"

"I'm good, little buddy. How are you holding up?"

"I'm fine, Dad. Everybody is here except for Jordan. Where are you?"

"I'm still about fifteen miles out, son. I'll be there in an hour and a half. Have you heard from Jordan?"

"Yes. He should be here any time."

"Good. Would you call me back when he gets there so I'll know everyone is safe?"

"Sure, Dad."

"Thank you. You're doing good, Zach. Very good. You be sure and protect those silly women down there for me, okay?"

Zach looked at his mother and then at Joyce. Both smiled.

"Okay, Dad. Will do."

"Ask them both if they have anything they want to talk to me about."

Linda shook her head no. Joyce said, "Just tell him to be careful, and that everything is okay here."

Zach relayed the message, word for word.

"Thank you, son. I'm so very proud of you. And I love you so much."

"I love you too, Dad. See you soon."

Joyce left the two of them alone and went back downstairs to finish preparing the weapons. She went back to Scott's office closet and took a box from the shelf. She placed the box on Scott's desk chair and opened it, then removed belts and holsters for the handguns and slings for the rifles. There were also extra magazines and four boxes of bullets.

The belts were military surplus, olive drab web belts that the army had used for generations. Scott said he preferred them because of the range of accessories they carried. Like a policeman's belt, you could attach pretty much anything to them, from extra ammo pouches to canteens to flashlights.

Each belt contained a holster and three pouches for extra ammunition. Joyce began filling the magazines, then placing the full magazines into the pouches.

Once finished, she put one of the belts around her waist and adjusted it. Snug, but not too tight. She was surprised at how heavy it was.

She put one of the Glocks into her holster and secured the flap over it. Then she holstered the other two guns and carried one belt, along with an AR-15, up the stairs to check on the other two.

"How are things going up here?"

"Fine. Nothing going on."

"Good. That's what I was hoping."

She leaned the AR-15 against the headboard, next to the window, and handed the extra web belt to Linda.

"It's still in safe mode. You'll have to cock it if you think you might need to use it."

Linda understood and asked no questions. Scott had made sure they were both well trained in the use of both weapons. He was surprised to find they were both pretty good shots.

Joyce said, "I'll take my turn at the window now, if you want."

She was getting a little bit antsy. She wouldn't be quite comfortable until the whole brood was together.

The three made small talk for another twenty minutes when Joyce noticed two people trudging up the long hill toward the house.

They weren't far away, maybe a hundred yards or so, but with only the moonlight to aid her, it was hard to make out any details.

"Linda, come look. The one on the left. Is that Jordan?"

She moved aside to share the window with Linda, who stood beside her and lifted another blind.

"Darn sure walks like him. I think it is."

Linda keyed the microphone on her radio.

"Jordan, this is Mom. Is that you approaching the house?"

Nothing but static.

"Jordan, is that you, honey?"

Still nothing.

The pair continued to watch until the mysterious couple crossed the street, headed straight for the house. Linda went downstairs to open the door, and Zach took her place at the window.

Once he was close enough, Joyce could make out Jordan's facial features in the moonlight.

"It's Jordan, all right. But who in the world is with him?"

Zachary knew, and rolled his eyes.

"That's Sara, his girlfriend."

# -40-

Linda opened the front door and hugged her oldest son. Then she ushered the pair in and relocked the door.

"Mom, this is my girlfriend Sara. I know what you're going to say. But her parents are stranded in St. Louis, and I just couldn't leave her there all alone to fend for herself. I just couldn't."

"Hush, baby. It's okay. You did the right thing."

Linda hugged Sara and said, "Welcome, Sara. This whole thing isn't going to be easy on any of us. But you'll be safe."

She looked at Jordan again.

"You guys must be starved. Joyce made some sandwiches. They're in the fridge. Get something to eat, and then sit down and rest. I'll call your dad and let him know you're here. How come you didn't answer your radio?"

Jordan gave her a sheepish look.

"I dropped it. It slipped out of my hand and onto the pavement. I guess I broke it. I'm sorry."

"Oh, don't worry about it, sweetheart. It happens. We have extras."

She keyed her radio mike.

"Scott, this is Linda. Can you hear me?"

"Much better than last time. Any word from Jordan?"

"Yes, he's here now. Everybody is safe. Just waiting for you."

Scott, who had stopped just long enough to refuel his Gator, was relieved.

"Great news! I'll call you when I'm close, so you can open up that section in the back fence and let me in. Do you remember how to do that?"

"Yes. We'll be waiting for your call. Be safe."

She turned to Jordan and said, "We'll tell him about Sara when he gets here."

"You don't think he'll be mad, do you?"

"No, of course not. He'd have done exactly the same thing in your position. But we'll have to modify our plans a bit."

Sara suddenly felt guilty, like she was intruding where she didn't belong.

"I'm sorry. I don't want to be a burden…"

Linda went to her and wrapped her arms around her.

"Oh, you hush, dear. You're not a burden. You're one of us now."

Linda suddenly remembered watching an airplane fall from the sky just after the power went out, and became concerned. She sat down at the table with them, and tried not to show it.

"So, your folks are in St. Louis? When did you expect them to come back?"

"They were supposed to fly back next Tuesday. Now I guess that's not possible."

Linda breathed a silent sigh of relief.

"No, I'm afraid not. Do you have other family up there?"

"Yes, that's where most of my aunts and uncles live. That's why they're up there, to attend my great aunt's funeral."

"Well, as long as they have other family members up there, they can band together for safety. And you're safe with us. What about your other brothers and sisters? Are they in St. Louis with your parents?"

"I have no siblings. I'm an only child."

"So everyone is safe. And you don't have to worry about them. So the only problem is that they'll be worried about you. Did they give you any instructions on where to go in an emergency?"

"Yes, my mom told me to go to the Bennett house if anything happened to them. That I'd be safe there."

"Okay, good. So they will assume you're safely with the Bennetts and that they won't have to worry so much."

Jordan interjected.

"She wrote her parents a note and left it on the counter, in case they find a way to come back for her."

Linda smiled and said, "Good. That was a very smart move. Now we know that everyone is safe, and there's no reason to worry. Now all we have to focus on is getting ourselves up the mountain to the compound."

Duke started barking in the back yard again.

Linda went to Scott's office at the back of the house, closed the door behind her, and blew out the candle lighting the room.

Then she eased back the drapes and peeped through the window blind.

The neighbor's cat was back.

Duke's barking was a good thing, she decided. It would scare away any prowlers that might be out there, looking at the darkened house and wondering if there was anything worth stealing inside.

After all, there were plenty of other darkened houses on this and other surrounding streets. Why take the chance on a dog bite, when they could choose another house?

"Keep barking, Duke. Bark the night away."

She reclosed the draperies and pulled a lighter out of her pocket to relight the candle.

Then she rejoined Jordan and Sara at the dining room table.

"You guys put on miner's lights, but don't turn them on unless you need them. We've got a few spare batteries, but would be wise to try not to use them up."

Sara asked, "What's a miner's light?"

Linda handed her one.

"It's like a little flashlight that sits on the middle of your forehead. Put the strap around your head and pull it tight. The light will shine in the direction your head is facing.

"I'm going upstairs to relieve Joyce on guard duty. After you guys are well rested and fed, you can come up and relieve me if you want."

Linda went up the stairs and explained to Joyce that Sara came along because she had nowhere else to go.

"I suspected as much," Joyce said. "I know Jordan is a good kid, and that he'll always do the right thing. I'm glad he brought her along."

Zachary pouted just a bit.

"I don't know why he can bring a girlfriend, and I couldn't."

Linda looked at her youngest son.

"Since when do you have a girlfriend, young man?"

"Aw, Mom. I've always had a girlfriend. She just never knew it. Until today."

Linda smiled. "But she knows now?"

"Yes. I told her I loved her. And then I kissed her. In front of the whole class."

He smiled broadly, obviously proud of himself.

Then his smile turned to a frown.

"Do you think she'll be okay?"

"Yes, sweetheart. Her family will go for her, and they'll take good care of her."

"Do you think I'll ever see her again?"

Joyce had to turn away.

Linda fought hard to hold back the tears.

"I'm sorry, Zach. I could lie to you, but the truth is you'll probably never see her again except in your dreams and your memories."

"Well, at least she knows that I love her. I guess that's something."

# -41-

At just before 10 p.m., the radios once again crackled to life.

"Joyce, Linda, this is Scott."

"Go ahead, Scott. This is Joyce."

"How's everything going there?"

"Good. Everyone is here now and we're just waiting for you. Are you getting close?"

"Yes. I'm a couple of miles away. Do you remember how to open the access in the back fence?"

"Yes. We'll be standing by. Let us know when you're within sight of it."

"10-4. Should be twenty minutes or so."

Joyce looked across the dining room table at Jordan and Sara.

"You guys want to help?"

Jordan spoke for both of them.

"Sure. Count us in."

The three went into the backyard and walked over to the back fence. It was a typical six foot privacy fence, with three horizontal two by fours stretching between fence posts, and wooden slats hammered onto the two by fours.

The fence looked like every other one in the neighborhood.

But looks can sometimes be deceiving. Scott had made some modifications to this particular fence several months before. It had a secret gate.

On the back part of the fence, which separated the yard from the woods behind the housing development, Scott had taken a hand saw and cut free a section of the fence.

Then he put the section back, held into place by six sliding bolts, similar to those securing front doors all over the world.

To remove the section of fence, one merely had to lift up each bolt lock and slide it over. It took about twenty seconds or so.

Then it was just a matter of moving the piece of fencing aside, leaving a hole just wide enough to drive a quad runner through. In this case, the Gator that Scott was feverishly driving down the mountain.

Scott had taken Joyce and Linda into the back yard after the modifications were done and showed them how to remove the section.

"Well, that's simple enough," Linda had said. "But what are the wire cutters for?"

She was referring to a new pair of wire cutters that Scott had wrapped in a zip lock bag, then placed inside a second ziplock bag, which was hammered to an adjacent fence post.

He could have just told them what the cutters were for, but he opted to show them instead.

He unlocked all six of the sliding bolts and moved the fence section to one side. On the other side of the fence, the girls saw three strands of barbed wire. The land behind the house had once been a cattle ranch, and the rusty wire once kept cattle from straying too far. Now it was just another obstacle in their way. But the wire cutters would take care of that problem.

Joyce had asked, "Why not just cut the wire now and be done with it?"

Scott said, "Well, I thought about that. But I figured if anyone ever got nosy and looked to see why the wire was cut, they might notice the cuts I made to the fence pieces. Also, the land belongs to the power company now, and they probably want to leave it up to keep people and vehicles out. So if I did cut it, they might just come around and repair it again."

Joyce was relating the story to Sara when Scott came over the radio again.

"Joyce, this is Scott. I'm about a minute away."

"10-4. We'll be ready."

Joyce and Jordan unlocked the fence panel and moved it to the side. Then Jordan took the wire cutters, snipped the barbed wire, and kicked the three strands out of the way.

They heard Scott's Gator approaching and stepped out of the way of the void that they'd created. He was running without lights, so they couldn't actually see him until he was twenty feet away.

When he neared the others, he slowed to a crawl, and then crept through the hole in the fence. He drove into the center of the yard, killed the engine, and removed his night vision goggles.

By the time Scott walked over to the fence to help replace the panel, it was already back in place.

He gave Sara a puzzled look. She was the last person he expected to see.

"Well, hello there. Sara, right?"

"Yes, sir."

Joyce took Scott's hand.

"Jordan brought her here because her family is out of the state. She was all alone. He did what you would have done under the same circumstances."

If they expected Scott to be angry about Sara's presence, they had him pegged wrong.

He merely smiled and said, "Well, then. Welcome to the family."

Then he looked at his son and said, "You understand that your mother and Joyce and I will be ganging up on you and watching you two like a hawk, right?"

Jordan corrected his father.

"Shouldn't that be like hawks?"

"Whatever. Just be sure you behave yourself."

"We will. I promise."

# -42-

Scott got settled and the group gathered in his bedroom. Jordan stood watch at the window and the others sat on the bed or stood.

Linda asked him, "What's the game plan?"

"Well, we need to move under cover of darkness. But it'll take some time to prepare, and it's too late to move out tonight. We'll stay the night here and rest up. Tomorrow we'll get everything ready, and at sundown tomorrow night we'll set out."

"How long will it take to get up there?"

"We could make it in five hours if we hauled ass. But we'd have to run the engines all out, and anybody within a hundred yards would hear us coming in time to try to stop us. So we're going to creep up there instead."

Zachary asked, "What do you mean, 'creep?' You mean like my brother?"

Jordan punched him in the arm.

"No, smartass. The nice thing about the Gators is they are almost silent when you take your foot off the gas and just let them creep along on their own. On open ground, the sound of the twigs breaking under the tires actually makes more noise than the engine itself. And we'll be driving on a gravel road, which will make even less noise.

"I want to get up there as stealthily as possible. Like ninjas. We'll go in the darkness, using night vision goggles to see. We'll use hand signals to communicate, or will whisper if we absolutely have to. And we'll creep so that the vehicles make little or no noise.

"We have to remember that there will be people out and about. Hunters will be out looking for game, and there may be outlaws out looking to steal whatever they can. Vehicles that actually work will be better than gold to them. That's why we have to be so careful."

"How long will it take to get there by creeping? Can we make it in one night?"

"I wish I could tell you yes, but I'm afraid I can't. Going at that speed, it'll likely take two full nights to get up there. I've got a great place scouted out to spend the day when the sun comes up. It's right at the halfway point. Very well hidden. We can drive the Gators off the road and into the woods and camp there while we wait for the night to return. In fact, the camping gear is already there. I dropped it off on the way down, so we'd have more room in the Gators going back."

"What about Duke?"

"Duke will follow us, and when he gets tired he can ride in the back. If he senses that someone is out there, he can alert us to their presence."

"But what if the outlaws hear him barking?"

"It doesn't matter. I always watch the weather forecast to see what the moon's going to do. At least I used to, before the power went out. I checked the ten day forecast the night before last. The next two nights will be partly to mostly cloudy with no moon. Very little light. So the bad guys may hear Duke barking, but they won't be able to see him. They'll likely think he's just a stray dog out looking for something to eat. In fact, in all likelihood they'll make an effort to steer clear of him."

"What about tonight?"

"We'll need to break into shifts to watch the front of the house. Duke will guard the back for us. Whoever stays up tonight can sleep during the day tomorrow while we do all the preparations."

Joyce said, "I'll take the first watch. My adrenaline's still pumping too much to let me sleep anyway. Anybody want to keep me company?"

Linda said, "I will. It'll give us a chance to catch up on our girl talk. We can keep each other from falling asleep."

Scott was okay with that arrangement. After the all day jarring trip down the mountain, he was exhausted and needed some rest.

Linda turned to Sara.

"Come with me, sweetie. I'll get you settled in the guest room."

Then she turned to Jordan.

"And after you tell Sara good night tonight, the guest room is off limits to you. Do you understand, young man?"

"Yes, ma'am."

Scott and the boys let the ladies have the honor of using what was left of the hot water still in the hot water heater. Once it was gone, they washed up with chilly water in the bathroom sink.

An hour later Linda and Joyce moved from Scott's room to an adjacent bedroom at the front of the house so that Scott could get some rest. He was asleep as soon as his head hit the pillow.

## -43-

Scott woke up the next morning to the smell of bacon frying. He stumbled to the kitchen.

Linda had retrieved a propane camping stove from the garage and was cooking what she could from the refrigerator.

To keep the fumes from becoming a problem, she slid open the patio door and placed the stove in front of it. On the other side of the screen door, Duke was lying forlornly, watching the bacon and licking his chops.

"Don't worry, boy. You'll get some too, I promise."

He wagged his tail, as though he understood every word.

She turned to Scott.

"I'm going to make all of the eggs we have left. There were three pounds of bacon in the chest freezer. I'm going to fry all of it and pack it into zip lock bags. We can snack on it on the trip up the mountain.

"I just tested the milk. It's still okay, but just cool now. Drink it before it sours."

"Do you think you guys can pack enough road food for two days?"

"Oh, sure. Joyce and I have already talked about it and we have a plan. There are several packages of lunch meat and three loaves of frozen bread in the freezer. We're going to leave it there until this evening, then we'll make it all into sandwiches. We've got two cases of water and a case of soda we'll take along, and we'll also take a few cans of ravioli and spaghettios in case anybody gets tired of sandwiches."

"Good. Just don't take anything we have to cook along the way. Campfires may attract the wrong kind of company."

Joyce came up behind him and hugged him.

"Linda, if you can spare a burner I'll boil some water for coffee."

"Oh, girl, that sounds great. Okay, the scrambled eggs will be ready in a couple of minutes. We can use that burner."

Scott turned around and kissed Joyce and said, "Sounds like you two have everything under control. How are the boys doing?"

"They're doing okay. They're all upstairs pulling guard duty together. And you really need to get used to calling them 'kids.' Not 'boys.'"

He remembered Sara and said, "Yes, I suppose so."

He looked at Joyce and said, "Do you think there's anything morally wrong about us taking her away from here? I mean, what if her parents find a way to get back eventually, just to find she's not here waiting for them?"

"In my opinion, it would be wrong if we *didn't* take her with us. I mean, the alternative is leaving a frail and vulnerable fifteen year old girl to fend for herself in what will soon be a very violent world. What chance would she have?"

He had to admit, she was right as usual.

"Besides, I talked to her last night. She left a note for her parents. It has our address in it so it will bring them to our house. I'm going to write a second letter for them today. I will tell them that when they get here, to make themselves at home. I will tell them that we have taken their daughter to a safe place, and that we will take good care of her.

"And I will also tell them that at some point, when we believe it's safe to do so, we will return her to them."

"Good. I slept like a rock last night. Did I miss anything? Was there any activity in the street?"

Linda spoke up again.

"No, the street was deathly quiet. We heard a lot of gunshots, but they were far away, over in the business district. We also saw a couple of yellow glows on the horizon. Fires, I suppose."

Joyce added, "We assumed it was probably looters, stealing whatever they could from the stores before the lights came back on. Imagine how stupid they'll feel when those huge televisions they carted away are absolutely worthless."

"Or it may be that the rioting has begun. That would explain the fires."

"It'll be twice as bad tonight. By then people will be furious with the power company, for not having service restored yet. And they'll be frustrated and sick of being stuck in their homes. I'm glad we won't be here to see it."

"How are you two holding up?"

"I'm beat. After we eat breakfast, Linda and I are going upstairs to crash. Y'all can wake us up in the afternoon to start preparing the food. Or before then if you need our help with something else."

"I don't think that'll be a problem. We've got all day long to make preparations. If you're still asleep at five, we'll wake you up then. I can't wait to get the hell out of here."

Scott said, "I'm going upstairs to relieve the kids so they can come and eat. After they're finished, would you have one of them bring me a plate?"

He headed up the stairs to find Jordan standing at the window watching the street, and Zachary and Sara sitting on the bed playing "rock, paper, scissors."

"Good morning you guys. How'd everybody sleep?"

"Pretty good, Dad. I sure was sore when I got up, though. I hope I never have to walk that far again."

"I think that's a safe bet. Are you guys hungry?"

"Starved."

"Well, head downstairs. Breakfast will be done soon."

"Dad, what's the game plan?"

"This afternoon we're going to get the vehicles ready and packed, and as soon as it's dark, we're going to head out. We'll go very slowly, and it'll take two full nights to get there. During the day in between we'll camp in the woods."

"So what's our job? Today, I mean?"

"There will be plenty to do. Your mom and Joyce will be making sandwiches and other food later and packing the coolers. You can help them. Or you can help me get the Gators ready to go. One of the things I want everybody to do is to eat as much as they can before we set out."

Jordan, who loved to eat, smiled and said, "Really?"

"Yes. Anything we leave behind will either spoil or be looted once our neighbors start running out of food. And the more we eat before we leave, the less hungry we'll get on the way, and the less food we'll have to pack for the trip. So find out what your mom and Joyce are setting aside for the trip and leave that alone. Everything else is fair game."

The kids went downstairs and Scott stood watch at the window. He watched several of his neighbors, assembled in the street three houses over.

He was tempted to go over and warn them. To tell them that the power wouldn't be coming back on today, as everyone hoped. That it would be many years before it came back on again. And that the world would become a very harsh and unforgiving place in the meantime.

But then he thought better of it. They likely wouldn't believe him. And they'd find out for themselves soon enough.

## -44-

Jordan and Sara sat together at the dining room table, chowing down on bacon and eggs.

Zachary sat across from them, picking at his.

Linda came up behind them and put an arm around each of them.

"How are you guys doing?"

"Fine, Mom. How come eggs always taste better when they're cooked on a camp stove?"

"You noticed that too? I've always believed that. And I don't know why. It's all in our heads, I suppose. Like maybe we associate a camp stove with vacations, or fun. I don't know. But they are good eggs, aren't they?"

Sara asked, "Is this the last time we'll ever have eggs?"

Linda smiled.

"Oh, no, sweetheart. Today, have Jordan tell you all about the compound and the preparations we've made up there. We've got hens for laying eggs and a milk cow, and other cows and pigs and chickens for meat. We've also got rabbits and a pond for fishing. It won't be paradise, but we'll have it a lot easier than most people."

Then she realized that what she said could have caused some pain.

"Oh, I'm sorry, Sara. I know you're worried about your parents. They'll be fine as long as they are with others and can help protect each other. I'm glad they have plenty of family up there in St. Louis. They can help each other survive. And I hope they can find a way to come back for you."

Sara got a strange look on her face.

"Yes. I hope so too."

"Honey, after you eat breakfast, I want you to come upstairs with me. You and I are about the same size, and you'll need clothes. I have a closet full of my things that I leave here. I want you to go through them and pick out what you want to take with us."

"Won't you need them?"

"No. I've got several boxes of clothes already at the compound. You're welcome to those too. I was going to leave my clothes here behind, but you'll need things to wear in case it's a few days before we can go through boxes. So you're welcome to anything you find."

Jordan chuckled.

"Just what I need. A girlfriend in mom clothes."

"Oh, you hush!"

Joyce went through the house, blowing out candles and opening each of the blinds a few inches to let in the morning sunshine.

She said, "Today is going to be a very memorable day, and for all the wrong reasons. Are you guys all okay?"

"Yep," Zachary said. "Fine as wine."

Jordan punched his brother on the arm.

"How would you know anything about wine, you little twerp?"

Zachary hit him back.

"I know as much about wine as you know about anything, you big ugly jerk."

Linda stopped the war before it got out of hand.

"All right, you two. Stop it. Finish your breakfast before I beat you both."

A bit later, Linda took Sara upstairs to go through the closet in the back bedroom. She and Scott hadn't been married in several years, but since Scott told her of the disaster to come, she kept a closet full of clothes and other personal items here. Just in case she was trapped in the house for any length of time.

As they were going through the closet and trying things on, Sara broke the ice.

"Linda, thank you for being so understanding."

"It's not a problem, honey. Really."

"I sort of have a confession to make."

"I know, honey. I'm ready, whenever you're ready to talk about it."

"You know? But how?"

"I'm a mom, Sara. As soon as we mentioned your family, I saw something in your eyes. Something that said you had a secret you were keeping. I don't know what it is, but whatever's the problem, I can't help you until it's out in the open."

Sara looked down. She didn't know where to begin.

"My parents won't be coming here looking for me."

It wasn't what Linda was suspecting. She was expecting the revelation that Sara and her son had been intimate, were lovers, or maybe even that a baby was in their future. But not this.

"But why?"

"Jordan was telling you the truth when he said I left my parents a letter. But I deceived him. All I really did was take an empty envelope and write their names on the outside of it."

Linda could see the pain in the young girl's eyes. But she didn't push her for answers. She waited until Sara was ready to say the words.

"I don't want my parents to come after me. I've been trying to get away from them for a long time. This is finally my opportunity."

"Have they been hurting you, honey?"

She held out her arms, and Sara came to her. Then the tears started flowing. First from Sara's eyes. Then from Linda's.

"He's not really my father. My real father left when I was five. I don't even know where he is. My mom said he died in a prison somewhere. But I haven't believed anything my mom has told me in years.

"My step-father... Jesse... he's not a nice man."

She paused, trying to find the words. Linda held her close and ran her fingers through Sara's long brown hair.

"It started out with Jesse coming to me in the night and touching me. Then it got worse. My mom drinks. She's been an alcoholic since before my real dad left. In fact, I think that's why he left.

"Mom and Jesse used to fight all the time about her drinking. Then he stopped. He told her he didn't care. Now it's almost like he encourages her to drink. Because two or three times a week, she gets way drunk and passes out.

"And that's when he comes to me."

"Does she know?"

"Yes. I've told her. She calls me a liar. She says he wouldn't do that. Then she tells me I must never tell anyone my 'lies' about Jesse. Because then they'll throw Jesse in prison. And she says that Jesse is a good worker, and he makes good money. And if Jesse gets locked up we won't have nice things, like a big house and nice furniture and flat screen TVs."

Sara looked at Linda. Then she looked down in shame.

"My mother turned me into a whore for her booze and for fancy television sets."

Linda put her fingers under Sara's chin and lifted up her face.

"Don't look down, honey. You've done nothing wrong. Don't you dare accept that man's shame for him. You are not a whore. You are a child. A child who has been terribly abused. But those days are over now, I promise you that. That animal will never abuse you again."

# -45-

Linda and Sara finished looking through clothes and removed several items from the closet. Linda found a box and they filled it up and wrote Sara's name on it.

"Remember, this is just to tide you over for the next few days. Once we're at the compound, you're more than welcome to go through the clothes I have there and claim whatever suits you. Now, how old are you, exactly?"

"Fifteen. I'll be sixteen in May."

"Okay, you may not be finished growing yet. If you grow a bit more and my clothes no longer fit you, I'm positive that Joyce will share hers. She's a size larger than me in some brands, and two sizes in others..."

Linda looked at Sara and saw tears in her eyes, and stopped talking immediately.

"What's the matter, dear?"

Sara reached out and hugged her, and held her close.

"Thank you so much for doing this for me. You had every right to send me away. Yet you're treating me better than my own mother has treated me in a very long time. And there is no possible way I can ever repay you."

"Shhhhh. You're wrong. We could never have sent you away. You were a very special part of Jordan's life, and now you're a very special part of ours. And no one will ever ask you to repay anything. You are one of us now, and we share easily. I know. I was an outsider too. Scott and I have been divorced for many years. He and Joyce could very easily have sent me away too. At first I thought they only invited me along because my sons insisted on it. But then I saw that they did it because they saw it as the right thing to do. They are good people, and none of us will treat you as an outsider. Now wipe those tears away, okay?"

Linda made a silly face and made her smile.

"However," Linda said. "Back to that other thing. Another thing we don't normally do around here is keep secrets. Under the circumstances, we're going to make an exception this time. But there will come a time when you will have to tell Scott and Joyce what you told me. Otherwise, they will start making plans to reconcile you with your parents again. They'll probably go through a lot of effort, and maybe even some risk, figuring out how to get your parents up there or you back to them in a safe environment.

"When you make it clear to them that you don't like the idea, but don't tell them why, the truth will come out. And then you will have destroyed their trust. And trust is something that you usually can't get back.

"So I'll keep your secret for the time being, but you'll need to start trying to find a way to tell them."

"Would you tell them for me?"

Linda thought hard.

"It's something that should come from you. I want you to try. But if you just cannot bring yourself to do it, then I will tell them for you."

"Okay. But no one will tell Jordan, right? I mean, I just couldn't bear for him to know."

Linda saw a look of mild panic on Sara's pretty face that she couldn't understand.

"Why, honey?"

"When no one is around, when we talk on the phone late at night… or when we used to… he would call me his little angel. I like that. He thinks of me as innocent and pure. And I haven't felt that way in a very long time."

The tears returned, and Linda held her.

"My ultimate dream is to marry Jordan someday. He is the most wonderful boy I've ever met. I want him to be mine forever. But if he knows I'm damaged goods…"

Her voice cracked. She couldn't continue.

"Shhhhhh. You're not damaged goods, honey. And if Jordan wants to think of you as his little angel, then he's absolutely right. In my opinion, he's not talking about your body or how pure you are. He's talking about the way you behave, the way you act, the way you make him smile and feel like's he's the most important guy in the world.

"And my son is brilliant. He's almost always right. So if he considers you an angel, then that's good enough for me."

She held Sara by the shoulders and looked her right in the eyes.

"And that thing I said about not keeping secrets around here? That only applies to grownups and to angels. Not to teenage boys. I mean, let's be real. Teenage boys are just barely human. Am I right?"

Sara chuckled.

"So let's make a deal. You try to find a way to tell Scott and Joyce so they don't waste a lot of time and trouble trying to reconcile you with your folks. If you honestly can't bring yourself to tell them, then I will for you. The three of us will keep your secret from Jordan and Zachary. And you can take that secret to the grave with you if you wish, or you can tell Jordan sometime later. Fair enough?"

Sara cried a few more tears, which didn't surprise Linda at all. She was a bit taken back, though, by Sara's next words.

"Thank you, Linda. I love you."

Now it was Linda's turn to tear up.

"You're welcome, dear. And I love you too."

# -46-

At mid-morning, Scott asked everyone to meet in the upstairs bedroom where Joyce was keeping watch.

"I've looked over everything, and it appears to be in good shape. I've also prepared a checklist of things we have to do, preparations we have to make, before we head out tonight.

"By my reckoning, it'll take about three hours to prepare everything if we break down into two teams. The guys can help me outside, if you ladies can work inside. We'll leave the patio door open, and Duke can have the run of the house. He'll alert us if he senses anybody out front, so we can stand down on guard duty.

"The sun should set around eight o'clock or so. That's when we'll set out, if everything is ready.

"Now, here's the kicker. I know everyone's all excited, and the adrenaline is flowing. But we're going to be up all night, the next two nights. It would be wise if everyone at least tried to take a nap."

Jordan spoke up.

"I already had one, when Zachary relieved me from guard duty this morning. I'm fresh. I'll take over the watch while you guys grab some sleep."

Scott admired his son for stepping up to the plate. He was becoming more and more of a man as each day went by.

"Good job, son. Did you remember to wind your watch?"

"Yes, sir."

"Okay, good. I don't expect any prowlers as long as it's light outside, but if I'm wrong, wake me up immediately. Otherwise you can wake us all up at five."

Scott laid down, Joyce at his side. He suspected it was a worthless cause, but he tried anyway. He dozed a couple of times, but never got any real sleep. There were just too many things running through his mind.

Jordan stood at the window, watching the street below him. There were a lot of things going through his mind as well. He felt sad for Sara, for having to leave her family behind. He had never been in love before, not really. But he was convinced that he was with this girl. He wondered how living together under the same roof would affect their relationship. As they walked the day before, down a lifeless highway strewn with disabled cars and frightened people, she had teased him.

"Maybe if we live in the same house for awhile, you'll start thinking of me as more of a sister type than a girlfriend. Maybe you'll lose interest in me, and when the time comes to marry you'll say you don't want to."

He'd stopped her and looked at her.

"No way," he'd said. "Living together will only bring us closer."

It was a claim he had no business making. The truth was, he didn't know what tomorrow would bring, much less the distant future. And he had no clue how their feelings would change in the months and years ahead.

All he knew was that, at this time and in this place, he loved this girl. And he was all she had now. He'd do his level best to prove himself worthy.

The street outside was dead. Every once in a while, a neighbor would come out and look around, as though watching out for the trucks from the power company that would be coming to their rescue. Trucks that should have come long ago but didn't. Trucks that some were starting to suspect were never coming again.

Still, it seemed that the more optimistic, or perhaps more naïve, kept their hopes alive.

Invariably, the neighbors who did journey outside to look around would shake their heads and slowly go back into their homes. Back into hiding. Back into hoping someone would rescue them from whatever in the world was going on.

Jordan was puzzled by the lack of children playing outside. They were lots of kids who lived on the block. Any other day before the blackout, they'd be all over the place. Riding their bikes and skateboards up and down the sidewalks. Playing football in the street. Playing basketball in their driveways.

But today, nothing.

Jordan wasn't sure if it was because their parents saw the danger of playing outside in this new, uncertain world, and perhaps had banished them to their back yards or indoors.

Or, perhaps they were still trapped at whatever schools they attended when the lights went out the day before. Perhaps the schools went on lockdown and were holding the students until their parents came for them.

And perhaps their parents lived or worked so far away, they couldn't come for them.

Jordan kept a close watch on the time, and at five o'clock sharp, he reached over to his little brother, who was sleeping peacefully in the bed beside him.

He grabbed his brother's shoulder and said, "Zach! Zach! It's time to get up."

Zachary stopped his soft snoring, snorted a couple of times, and opened his eyes.

He was wide awake and out of bed in seconds. He wanted to get this show on the road. He was tired of being cooped up in this house, worried about being attacked and maybe killed by marauders.

He went to his Mom's room and shook her by the shoulder.

She opened an eye and said, "Well, hello, little man."

"Hi, Mom. It's time to get up."

"Nope. I cannot possibly get up until I have a hug from my son."

"Aw, Mom…"

"Aw, Mom nothing. Come on. It won't hurt you."

He laid his head on her shoulder and put his arm around her waist.

"Mom, are we really going to be okay?"

"Of course, honey. Why do you ask that?"

"I kinda had a bad dream. That we were on our way to the compound and somebody started shooting at us."

"That can't happen, honey. That's why we're going at night. Nobody will be able to see us. At least, unless they planned ahead like we did and protected night vision goggles and batteries. And that's probably not very likely."

"Mom, I love you."

"I love you too, honey. Did you wake everybody else?"

"Nope. You were the first."

"Thank you for the hug, sweetie. Now run along and wake everyone else, okay?"

Zach was off like a shot to Sara's room. He stood in the darkened doorway and said, "Sara, are you awake?"

"Yes. Is it time?"

"Yes."

She arose and followed Zach to Scott's bedroom. It was empty. Scott and Joyce were already downstairs, preparing dinner. Joyce had a pot on the camp stove, boiling spaghetti noodles. On the auxiliary burner she was heating up a can of Ragu. It wasn't the fanciest of dinners. But it was food, and it would help fill their stomachs for the long journey.

Joyce took the noodles off the burner and drained them in the sink. Then she tasted the sauce, declared it done, and placed it on the counter.

"Okay, you guys dig in. This will be the last hot meal you get for two days, so eat up."

While everyone else sat down to eat, Joyce opened the back door and let Duke in. For the rest of the evening, he was their security system.

## -47-

Scott finished his dinner first, having fairly wolfed it down so he could get started.

"I'm going outside. You boys join me when you're finished."

He looked at Linda, then at Joyce.

"You girls know what to do?"

"Yep."

Joyce looked at Sara.

"Sara, would you mind helping us?"

"Sure."

Jordan and Zachary followed their father into the back yard, and Sara, anxious to earn her keep and prove her worth, asked, "What can I do?"

"Why don't you grab those four large coolers in the den and bring them in here?"

Sara did as asked, and Linda gave her more instructions.

"There are a couple of cases of bottled water over there by the refrigerator and a case of sodas. We want two coolers to be water and one cooler to be sodas.

"If you'll leave some room at the top of each of the coolers, you can go out into the garage to the chest freezer. There are about twenty or so frozen blocks of blue ice you can top off the coolers with. That'll keep the drinks cold for at least a day, maybe longer.

"Once they're full, don't try to carry them. Just drag them over to the back door and let the guys know they're ready and they can come get them. Might as well let them put those muscles to work."

Sara set about her project while Linda and Joyce started making sandwiches. They made a variety, using up all of the lunch meat and fresh produce in the refrigerator. They also boiled three packages of hot dogs, rolled each of them in a slice of white bread, added a line of mustard, and sealed each one in a zip-lock snack bag. The boys loved mustard dogs, and they'd wolf these down two or three at a time.

Once the sandwiches were done and packed in a cooler, they made a huge tossed salad. They split it up into roughly equal portions and put the portions in twelve zip-lock sandwich bags, added assorted flavors of salad dressings into each bag, and shook them up.

Joyce took a black sharpie, and on each bag she wrote either an "F" for french dressing, an "I" for italian, or an "R" for ranch. Then she looked at the bags and laughed at her wasted efforts. It was easy to tell the difference even without her marks. The salads went in the cooler on top of the sandwiches.

While Joyce was marking the salads, Linda went to the garage and got four blocks of blue ice to keep the food cold. When the cooler was finally closed, the women each took one handle and carried it over to the back door.

Sara finished her task and asked for more to do.

Linda said, "There are three laundry baskets stacked together in the laundry room, dear. Take them into the cupboard. Fill them up with whatever snacks you want to take for the trip. Enough snacks for seven people and one dog for two days. You decide what to take. There are potato chips in there, and cookies, and breakfast and granola bars, and all kinds of other stuff."

Sara disappeared, and Joyce commented, "What a sweet and helpful girl. I think I'm going to enjoy having her as part of the family."

While the girls were making their preparations, the guys had work of their own. Scott had opened the large storage building that doubled as a Foley cage and had driven the two additional Gators out into the back yard, where he lined them up behind the one he brought off the mountain.

When he bought the all wheel drive vehicles, he had the option of getting them with four wheels and a short bed, or with six wheels and a longer bed. He chose the longer beds. They'd carry a lot more cargo. They also had a larger engine, which would help them get up the mountain easier when fully loaded.

"Okay, Zach, you take the double air mattress and blow it up, but not all the way. Blow it up about halfway, and then wedge it into the bed of the first Gator. Then go into the house and get a couple of blankets and a pillow. Somebody's going to have to pull guard duty tomorrow at the camp, while everybody else is sleeping. They'll have to get some sleep in tonight."

"Jordan, the middle Gator will be our food supply. Go get all the coolers and stuff that the girls are putting by the back door and load them up. Put the coolers on the outside, so it's easier to get drinks along the way."

Scott opened the hoods on the Gators and checked their oil and water levels. The batteries were sealed, but almost new, so he expected no problems with them. He also did a thorough inspection to make sure all the belts were tight, none of the hoses were hard or brittle, and nothing looked amiss. They all appeared to be in top working order.

He closed the hoods and went into the garage. Weeks before he'd bought rear view mirrors for the driver's side of each vehicle. He'd never gotten around to installing them, but it wouldn't take long. The Gator's hood was made of a heavy plastic instead of steel to reduce its weight. Even without a working drill, he could force screws in to hold the mirror in place, just by applying pressure as he turned them. It was essential that the drivers be able to keep track of each other. In the darkness, it would be easy to get separated, and the mirrors would make it easier to keep the back vehicles in view. That way the slower vehicles wouldn't get left behind along the way.

Scott reached under the dash of each of the vehicles and removed the fuses for the headlights, tail lights and brake lights. Lights would be a beacon that would alert others for hundreds of yards that they had working vehicles. They were therefore a major liability.

And they didn't need lights anyway. They had night vision goggles, which would amplify the light from the stars and enable them to see.

Jordan finished loading the coolers and food, and asked, "Okay, what next?"

"Take the night vision goggles and install the batteries. The battery box is at the very top, on the inside. They take four AA batteries, if I remember right. There are several boxes of batteries next to them. It'll be dark within the next twenty minutes or so, and you can test them out when you're done. Also, you can get that blue box off the back of the second Gator. You'll like what you find in it."

"Oh, I will, huh?"

"Yep."

"Well, how about if I open it first then?"

"Nope. If you open it first, you might not get the batteries in the night vision goggles before it gets dark. Besides, what's in the box is your reward for putting the batteries in without screwing it up. You can't have the reward until your mission is done."

He looked at Jordan and smiled.

Jordan grinned and said, "Sheesh…"

Zach finished making a bed in the back of the first Gator and returned for more instructions.

"Go ask the girls if they've got all of their stuff packed, and bring it out and put it in the last Gator. Leave room at the back of the bed for Duke, though. Throw his bed and blanket, food bowl and water dish in the very back. But make sure the dishes are empty. Then take his bag of dog food and put it in the back as well."

Twenty minutes after sundown, they were ready to go. Everyone had their goggles on, and was looking around in amazement at the view they cast.

Sara asked, "How come everything is so green?"

Scott explained, "They take the available light from the stars above and amplify it. Green is the color they found that amplifies it the best."

Zachary looked at Jordan through the green lens.

"Boy, do you look like a dork in that thing."

"Yeah, like you look any better."

"You guys stop. Jordan, did you ever open that blue box I gave you?"

"Oh, no, I forgot about it."

He opened it up and said, "Hey, cool! MP-3 players! But how come they're so big?"

"They're battery operated. They don't need a computer to recharge. When they go dead, you just replace the AAA batteries. I figured you guys would need them to keep from being bored on the trip."

"Cool. What kind of music did you put on them?"

"All country. Waylon and Willie mostly. The good stuff."

All three of the kids looked at him. The goggles hid their expressions, which was probably a good thing. Zach's jaw had dropped.

Scott laughed.

"I'm just kidding. It's all of that rap and pop and other crap you guys downloaded onto my computer."

The three appeared to breathe a collective sigh of relief.

"Now remember, once we leave the yard, no talking. If you want to talk to somebody, tap them on the shoulder, and then use hand signals. If they are close enough to you, whisper in their ear. But no talking. Talking is dangerous from here on out."

"Okay. Who's riding with who?"

"Zach will be riding in the first Gator with me. Jordan, you and your mom will be in the second Gator. Your mom has volunteered to pull guard duty when we camp tomorrow. That means she's going to be in the back of my Gator sleeping for a good portion of the trip. When she does, you can drive, and Sara can sit with you and keep you company. Otherwise, Sara, you can ride in the third Gator with Joyce."

"What about Duke?"

"Duke will follow us. You girls in the back keep an eye on him, and if he starts to lag, it's probably because he's tired. When that happens, Sara, you run up and tell me and we'll stop the convoy. Jordan can pick Duke up and put him on his bed to take a nap and rest."

"How fast will we be going?"

"Not fast. The Gators will creep along at about three miles an hour, maybe a bit more, in silent mode. The engines won't make any noise at all at that speed, and the only sound you'll hear is the occasional stick or leaf being crushed under the wheels. That's the safest way. It'll be too dark for anybody to see us, and if they can't hear us either, we should be able to get up the mountain without anyone trying to take our vehicles or food away from us."

Joyce added, "It's going to be a long hard trip, especially since we can't talk to each other. It's also going to be very boring. If you get sleepy, just step off the vehicle and walk for a bit. If you walk at a fast pace, you'll be able to stay up with your Gator and the walk will wake you back up again."

"Any questions?"

There were none.

"Okay, I'm going to take the fence section down so we can drive the Gators out. This will be your last chance to use a real bathroom for the next two days, so if anybody wants to go, I'd suggest you do it now."

Sara and Zachary immediately scrambled back into the house.

# -48-

By the time the kids did their business and rejoined the others, the three Gators were already idling in the large field behind the house. Zach and Sara ran through the opening in the fence and Scott replaced the panel, locking it into place. Then he climbed over the fence and hopped to the ground on the other side.

The convoy crept slowly through the brush to the long line of power poles, which stretched high into the night sky. Duke followed dutifully behind the vehicles, not sure where they were going and why, but happy to be out of the back yard.

Once they neared the power lines, the heavy brush gave way to mowed grass. The electrical coop had always gone a great job of keeping this area maintained, and it would work to the group's advantage.

They swung onto the road that ran directly under the towers. In the daytime, a week before, they would have been intimidated by the massive two hundred foot tall structures over their heads, with a dozen deadly electrical lines humming loudly.

Now, though, the lines were dead and silent. And the tall towers themselves were merely green tinted shadows.

As planned, the three drivers kept their feet off the accelerator pedals, and just let them creep along. They were virtually silent, except for the occasional crunch of something under one of the balloon tires.

The hardest part, of course, was the pace. It was dreadfully slow. Jordan stepped off of his Gator for several miles, walking alongside the one Sara was in so he could hold her hand along the way. In lieu of words, they exchanged hand gestures, blowing each other kisses and touching fingers to their hearts and pointing to the other.

Joyce, sitting next to Sara and driving the third Gator, enjoyed the spectacle. It reminded her of the days when she was young and in love, and desperate to express that love in every way possible.

It also reminded her that they'd have to keep a close eye on these two in the months ahead. To make sure they didn't go too far in finding ways to express their love for one another.

Joyce, bringing up the rear, was tasked to keep an eye on Duke as well. That was a bit harder than watching Jordan and Sara. Duke disappeared from view several times, but only for a couple of minutes each time. Joyce assumed it was to chase a rabbit or a cat, or perhaps to take a potty break. Each time, once the convoy was out of his view, he went romping back to catch up.

After two hours, Scott ground his Gator to a halt, and the others stopped directly behind him.

He opened up the large Igloo cooler and removed a bottle of water. He looked around at all the green faces watching him and made a pointing gesture to the cooler, asking if anyone else wanted one. He had a couple of takers, and passed them around.

Scott went to the back of the third Gator and grabbed Duke's water bowl from the back. He put it on the ground and poured a bottle of water in it. Duke lapped it up quickly. Walking apparently worked up a powerful thirst for him. And he was doing great thus far.

Scott lifted up each of his paws, one at a time, and felt the soft pads. He watched for Duke's reaction, to see if he winced when Scott touched a tender spot. Nothing. He felt no blisters or sores on the pads, and deemed the dog good to go until the next rest stop.

After ten minutes or so, everyone had a chance to stretch their legs, get something to drink and wander off to use the bathroom. It was time to set out again.

Linda tapped her oldest son on the shoulder and pointed to the driver's seat. Then she crawled into the back of the first Gator to take a nap while Jordan took the wheel.

Seeing this, Sara looked forlornly at Joyce. Her look required no interpretation. Joyce waved her off and she went to sit next to her boyfriend in the middle Gator. She held his hand as they waited to depart again.

Scott picked up Duke and laid him on his bed on the back of the Gator, in case he needed a rest.

But Duke wanted none of that. He was having too much fun. As soon as the convoy restarted, he jumped down and trudged along behind them again.

The next couple of hours were uneventful, even boring, and everyone was starting to let their guard down. Then, off in the distance, the group made out a brilliant light. They didn't know what it was, but the night vision goggles amplified the light to such a degree it was almost painful to look directly at it.

As they drew closer, and could hear voices in the distance, Scott stopped his vehicle and removed his goggles. In normal light, without the goggles, he could see that the brilliant light was a large campfire, a mere hundred yards away now, burning at the back of a large residential area adjacent to the power lines.

It appeared that someone was having a party, although Scott was at a loss to determine what they might be celebrating.

Perhaps it was a macabre "end of the world" party. Or maybe they finally recognized that once their beer got warm it might never be cold again. Maybe they were trying to drink it all up before it had a chance to warm.

Whatever the reason, their presence was a liability.

The campfire was east of the road the group was on, and perhaps fifty yards from it. In the darkness, Scott was almost certain that they could pass right by the partiers without being seen.

But almost certain wasn't good enough. Just as a precaution, Scott turned to his left and went over to the auxiliary road, which followed the power lines on their west side. This road wasn't as well maintained, and might make a bit more noise, but it was fifty yards farther away from the campfire.

And with all the whooping and hollering going on at the party. Scott didn't see the slightly more noise as much of a problem.

Scott motioned to Zachary to get out of the Gator and to walk alongside it on the driver's side, and to crouch down low.

Just in case.

He took the Glock out of his holster, switched off the safety, and chambered a round. Then he laid it on the empty seat beside him.

Just in case.

Slowly, they crept forward, past the group of laughing and drunken fools who were celebrating at one of the worst times of their lives.

Scott wondered why it is that the most ignorant can also be the most blissful.

After two hundred yards, the bright light from the campfire was growing more and more dim behind them, and the noise could no longer be heard.

Scott eased back over to the better road, directly underneath the mammoth towers, the others following closely behind him.

He stopped the convoy, put his handgun back on safe and back in his holster, and walked into the shrubs to use the bathroom. A couple of the others did the same.

Back at the vehicles, he got a bottle of water from one of the coolers and looked questioningly at everyone else. A couple of the others made gestures meaning more or less, "sure, I'd like one." So he passed water over to them.

Linda woke up, having missed the whole campfire ordeal. She'd been exhausted, and needed a few hours of good sleep. She'd need it even more the following day, when everyone else was sleeping and she was pulling guard duty.

Once everyone was back in their places, the convoy set out again.

Scott checked his watch. It was 4:30 a.m.

They had approximately two hours of darkness left.

He checked the number on the next tower as they drove underneath it. Tower number 18208. Their camping site was east of Tower 18421.

By his calculations, at the rate of speed they were going, they'd be at the campsite in an hour and a half.

Scott cursed himself that they'd get to the site with half an hour of darkness left. That was wasted travel time.

But it couldn't be helped. This whole thing wasn't an exact science, after all.

And, he supposed, he should just count his lucky stars that they were halfway home without incident.

But they still had a long way to go.

# -49-

Just as the distant sky showed signs of lightening up just a bit, the convoy drove slowly underneath Tower number 18421.

Once clear of the tower, Scott made a sharp right turn, and crept out of the short grass and into the scrub brush and mesquite trees that shadowed the power lines to the east.

Eighty yards away from the towers, the brush got thicker, and the shrubbery got higher. The mesquites were replaced by tall spruces and fir trees.

Scott made a left turn at a twisted fir he'd remembered from two days before, and drove into a flat meadow, perhaps the size of a football field.

He kept driving until he came to the pile of tents, sleeping bags, and blankets he'd left there on his way down the mountain.

He'd found this place on Google Earth several months before. It seemed to have everything they needed. The flat land was perfect for camping. The shrubs and scrub brush provided great cover. It even had a fast running stream running through it where they could wash up if they wanted to.

They parked the Gators in an arc, with the front of each one pointing more or less to the east. That way the beds on the back of each Gator would be closest to the tents, and the items in the beds would be easily accessible.

Ever the cautious soul, Scott called all of the others into a tight circle.

"We're pretty isolated now. There shouldn't be anyone else out here besides us, except maybe a hunter or fisherman or two. But just to be safe, keep your voices very low, okay?

Everyone understood.

Scott, Joyce, and Linda had set up these tents several times before at the compound, just to familiarize themselves with them.

They knew where every peg went, every pole was grounded, every flap attached. The others just stood back and watched.

In fifteen minutes there were three four man tents fully erect, and formed in another arc opposite the truck beds. Seen from above their campsite formed a perfect circle.

When Scott purchased the tents, he opted for four man tents instead of two. As any camper knows, tent manufacturers take a lot of liberties when it comes to determining how many bodies their tents will accommodate. A typical two man tent will only accommodate two men if they are the size of small women. Or if they like incredibly cramped spaces.

A four man tent, on the other hand, will provide two average sized adults room to stretch out and get comfortable when they sleep.

And he figured that after sitting upright in Gators all night long, everyone deserved to sleep a few hours in comfort.

Once the tents were up, the group massed in the center of the campsite and whispered to each other. They'd split up two to a tent. Scott and Joyce would take one, of course. Linda would be on guard duty, so Sara would have the middle tent to herself.

Jordan was disappointed that he couldn't share a tent with Sara.

Zachary was disappointed that he had to share a tent with Jordan.

They dared not build a campfire, for fear that the smoke or the smell might attract any curious people in the area. So instead they had sandwiches and tossed salads for breakfast. It was surprisingly tasty, perhaps because they'd had all night long to work up a hunger.

This day was cooler than it had been the day before. Or perhaps it just seemed that way because they were halfway up the mountain. And it was always five degrees cooler above the city.

In either case, Linda felt chilled, and pulled a sweatshirt out of her bag to put on over her other clothes.

While the others slept, she walked the perimeter of the meadow. It helped her stay awake, and gave her a chance to get some exercise and stretch her legs. When she got tired, she sat in the passenger seat of one of the Gators and watched out over the great expanse of the clearing.

She'd forgotten to wind her watch the day before, and was disheartened to see that it had stopped.

Scott was pretty good about looking at the position of the sun in the sky and judging the time of day. He could usually guess within half an hour either way. He told her once it was one of the vestiges of his youth, when a boy scout counselor taught his charges how to tell time from the position of the sun.

Linda, though, had no such talents.

She waited until the sun was directly over her head, wound her watch, and set it for twelve noon. She'd ask the first person to awaken what time it was and see how close she came.

She reflected about all they had gone through already, and everything that lay before them. She worried, too, about how hard the change in their lives would be for all of them.

She wondered whether she would be up to the task.

Then she decided she would be. After all, it hadn't even been a year before when she was nothing but a whipping post for Glen's anger, and she accepted the beatings she got as normal. She finally mustered the strength to tell him to go to hell, and walked away.

For a brief moment, she wondered where Glen was at that moment, and what he was doing.

And for even a briefer moment, she felt pity for him.

Then nothing.

She thought of the whole situation with Sara. She knew what it was like to be mistreated at the hands of bad men. Glen wasn't the first. She, more than anyone else, could relate to what Sara had gone through. Perhaps Sara sensed that, and that's why they had bonded so quickly.

She wondered if she should go ahead and tell Scott and Joyce what Sara had told her. So they could empathize with her too.

But no, it wasn't her place. She'd give Sara the chance to tell them in her own time, in her own way. That would be the proper way to handle it.

In the early afternoon, Duke took off like a bolt of lightning after a rabbit he sensed on the far side of the meadow. Back and forth they went, from one side of the meadow to the other. Each time Duke would get close, the rabbit would quickly change directions and bolt again.

Linda wasn't sure why the rabbit was toying with him, and wondered why it didn't just bolt for the brush.

Then she decided it was probably a mother, with babies in a nearby rabbit hole, who didn't want to abandon them.

She suddenly started rooting for the rabbit instead of Duke.

Then she took a closer look, and noticed that Duke wasn't running at full gallop. The scoundrel was merely playing with the rabbit, to have something to do. He meant the rabbit no harm.

And she wondered if the rabbit sensed that too. Perhaps the rabbit was also playing. Perhaps the things that animals do to interact with each other aren't always life or death. Perhaps they sometimes enjoy each other's company. Perhaps.

Finally, Duke got tired of the game and sauntered back over to Linda, his tongue hanging limply from his mouth. She refilled his water dish and watched as he noisily lapped it up. It was the first time she noticed his whiskers were starting to turn gray.

They'd bought a female black lab a few weeks before, and had taken her directly to the compound. They'd named her Duchess, of course. She looked a lot like Duke, and she'd make a fine bride.

Duchess was the surprise awaiting Duke when they made it to the compound.

Neither dog had been fixed. The hope was that they would be fruitful and provide the compound with playful, yet vigilant, guard dogs for generations to come.

And that thinking, of course, led Linda's thoughts back to the Jordan and Sara situation. And how to keep them from multiplying as quickly as Duke and Duchess.

She decided that they'd have to be watched extremely closely. At least until they could be trusted. And, seriously, who can ever really trust teenagers when it came to sex and abstinence?

When the sun was beginning its downward arc, Scott stumbled out of his tent and jogged over to the shrubs to use the bathroom. It dawned on Linda that she needed a similar respite, so when Scott returned she handed him the AR-15 and had him relieve her for a few minutes.

She kicked herself for not noticing that this was the first time all day that she'd felt a need to go. She knew that meant she was dehydrated. And she also knew that being dehydrated meant she wasn't on her best game. Pulling guard duty at anything less than fully alert wasn't smart and could have been dangerous.

She made a mental pledge to herself to drink more water from here on out, and to encourage everyone else to do the same.

After she returned from the shrubbery, she asked Scott what time it was. He looked at his watch and said "4:40."

She checked her own watch and was pleased to see she was only twenty minutes off.

He spoke to her in a voice barely more than a whisper.

"I'm up for the day. If you want, I'll take watch so you can grab a nap before we set out."

She pondered the idea and said, "I'd like that, but I think I'll have something to eat first."

He chuckled.

"Me too. I'm famished. That's what I came out here for."

Scott opened a can of ravioli, and ate it cold, out of the can, with a plastic fork.

Linda ate a ham and cheese sandwich, and a bag of Lay's chips, and washed her food down with two bottles of water. She expressed her concern about dehydration with Scott, who admitted that he too wasn't drinking as much as he should and vowed to do better.

They sat there together, the two of them, speaking in hushed tones about the past, and the future.

They'd been high school sweethearts so many years before. Had gotten married and had two children, and the usual problems encountered by people who have kids before they're completely grown themselves.

They'd had a lot of good times, and some bad times as well. But through it all they'd been able to remain great friends. And it wasn't just a show for the boys' sake, either. They still had whatever traits they'd had so many years before, when they first came together.

And both just took it for granted that the bond would always be there. That whatever happened or didn't happen in the years ahead, that they'd always be there for each other. To help each other through the rough spots, and to help celebrate the good.

After all, it had been that way for a very long time.

# -50-

In the twilight of the day, the rest of the group finally began to emerge. The first night's drive had taken a lot out of them, and exhaustion had set in. That wasn't necessarily a bad thing, since it helped them sleep easier on hard ground that was anything but comfortable. Now, though, as they came out of their tents, they were stiff and sore and needed to walk around a bit to make their muscles and joints stop hurting.

So one by one, they came out of the tents, like zombies, walking stiffly and silently in awkward steps, absent of grace or finesse. And one by one they loosened up, stretched, and acknowledged the others, with a smile or a wave or another gesture.

And one by one they went off to the brush to relieve their bladders, then to the coolers to fill their stomachs.

None of them, except perhaps Duke, were looking forward to another night's crawl up the mountain.

But every one of them was looking forward to getting there, and accepted the trip as essential to making that happen. So they took the blankets, folded them up and laid them across the Gators' seats, and accepted their fate. Perhaps tonight would go a little easier once they could see the light at the end of the tunnel.

Scott had even hinted that perhaps they could pick up the pace a little bit, since the second half of the trip was all wilderness. And that any hunters or fishermen on the mountain would probably be hunkered down for the night.

In the waning hours of sunlight, their bellies full and sleep replenished, they broke down the camp and stuffed the tents and sleeping bags into the beds of the Gators. Then it was just a matter of waiting.

Duke provided some comic relief when the fireflies came out. He'd never encountered them before, and didn't know what they were. He chased them across the meadow when they were alit, and then came to a screeching halt when their lights went out.

Each time a bug disappeared, he looked to his humans with a puzzled look on his face, as though he were asking them, "Where did it go?"

The group also shared a more tender moment.

Sara had never seen fireflies before either, and was fascinated by them. Jordan caught one for her, and the rest of the group watched from a distance as the young couple, with the setting sun behind them, peered with awe at the tiny creature cupped within his hands.

Joyce commented, "Those two are falling so much in love. I'm glad she was able to come along."

Zachary thought once again of Amy, the love of his own life, and thought it was patently unfair that she was missing from the group. Everyone else had someone. Even his Mom had Tom Haskins, the neighbor who lived not far from the compound. And Duke would soon have Duchess.

Zachary suddenly felt like the odd man out. He'd be moody in the coming hours, and no one would know why. They'd all just chalk it up to fatigue and the long journey. But in the night, as he looked up at the stars, he'd see Amy's face, and sob silently to himself.

# -51-

The second half of their journey went without incident. When they were five miles from their destination, Scott did some computations in his head. He wanted to arrive at the compound in the darkness. But to do that, they'd have to move at a faster pace. So for the last hour they doubled their speed.

It wasn't much of a concession, but it was welcomed by all. It was like a prize for a job well done. And for the first time since the journey began, they could feel a very welcome breeze wash gently across their faces.

As they neared the turnoff for the compound, Scott, still in the lead vehicle, once again slowed to a crawl.

A hundred yards later, when they reached the end of the compound's drive, he stopped completely and got off the Gator.

The others watched from a distance as Scott crawled around on hands and knees on the dirt road. They had no clue what he was doing, but trusted him enough to know there was an explanation for his odd behavior.

And indeed there was. On his way down the mountain, Scott had strung a light brown thread across the driveway, tied to rocks on each side. The thread was the same color as the roadway, about four inches above it, and was virtually invisible.

It was a makeshift alarm system. Anyone driving or walking into the compound in their absence would have broken the thread, and would have made entering a lot more difficult.

But Scott was relieved to discover that the thread was still intact. No one had gone beyond this point.

He was also happy to hear Duchess, barking menacingly to whoever or whatever she heard lurking in the darkness. If anyone had come this far, it was likely that Duchess would have scared them away.

She was a great dog, as was Duke. Scott looked forward to greeting their first litter of puppies.

He climbed back onto his Gator and led the group into the front yard of the fortified house. Then he stepped off one more time to unlock the gate of the high steel fence which surrounded the compound.

Immediately upon opening the gate, he was tackled by Duchess, who slobbered all over his face and wagged her tail madly, as though he'd been gone for a thousand years.

Duke came bounding over, first to protect his master from this threat, then to watch as he realized Scott was in no danger. Duchess noticed Duke almost immediately. She walked over to him and they performed the sniffing ritual that would mark the beginning of their very short courtship.

It so happened that Duchess was in heat. She and Duke would spend the next couple of days getting to know each other intimately.

The weary travelers parked their Gators in the yard and lumbered off of them, even more exhausted than they'd been the previous morning.

The house was darkened, having suffered the same fate as the rest of the world.

But no one really cared. They knew that in the days ahead, there was much to be done to give the house power again, and to get everything sorted out and situated for their permanent occupation. But for now, they just wanted to rest.

After a few hours of sleep, Scott would go into the darkened basement and remove a 10,000 watt generator from the wood and metal crate that had protected it from the solar storms. He'd vent it to the outside and crank it up.

While Scott was doing that, the rest of the group would crack open the wooden storage building, lined with metal, that held new televisions, DVD players, microwaves, and a dozen other appliances to replace the ones fried by the storms. And by the end of the second day at the compound, they would be living almost normal lives again.

But that would all come later. Right now, after their long journey, it was time to sleep.

The group headed into the house as the sun first started peeking over the horizon, shedding light on their new home. After two long nights of wearing the heavy night goggles, they were sick of them and threw them aside. Duke picked up one of them and took off like a bolt. He had plans to chew his new toy to pieces.

Duchess was right behind him, wanting to share his find. At first he was selfish and growled at her, to tell her it was his and his alone. Then he decided to share because, well, that's what boyfriends do with their girlfriends.

Scott, at first tempted to chase the dogs to get the goggles back, had second thoughts. He was too tired to run. And besides, he couldn't imagine the circumstances coming to pass where they'd need the goggles again. So he let them be.

Linda went through the house and opened all the curtains and blinds to let the sunshine in.

Then she read Jordan and Sara the riot act.

"Don't think you're being picked on, because you're not. But I know what it's like to be a teenager, with all of those hormones going on and weird things happening to your bodies. Even though you're not guilty of anything, you're still going to be treated like you are. It's nothing personal. It just is what it is.

"So, Sara, you and I are going to share the back bedroom for the time being. It's a big room, with its own bathroom, and two beds. I hope you don't mind. If it helps, I don't snore like your boyfriend does."

Sara went to Linda and held her.

"I don't mind at all. I'd love to be your roomie."

Then she looked at Jordan and asked, "You snore?"

Jordan turned red, and Linda could tell from Sara's reaction that she really hadn't known.

And she took some comfort in that.

They ate what was left of their travel food for breakfast. And by ten a.m., every one of them was sound asleep.

Except for Duke and Duchess, out in the yard. They were finding other things to do.

\*\*\*\*\*\*\*\*\*\*\*\*\*\*\*\*\*\*\*\*\*\*\*\*\*\*\*\*\*\*\*\*

I sincerely hope you enjoyed reading **Countdown to the Apocalypse.** It was a fun book to write.

The sequel, called **After the Dust Settled,** will be out in the summer of 2014. It will tell the story of life in the compound and the group's efforts to reach out to others. It will also answer the question on everybody's mind: Does Zachary get a girl of his own?

Please enjoy the following excerpt from **The Cleansing,** now available on Amazon.com and from Barnes and Noble Booksellers...

\*\*\*\*\*\*\*\*\*\*\*\*\*\*\*\*\*\*\*\*\*\*\*\*\*\*\*\*\*\*\*\*

Ron Bennett was a scumbag. Not in his own eyes, of course. He thought quite highly of himself. As a former President of the United States, he was well known, and people paid him lip service and told him how great he was everywhere he went. But they did that to every former President, simply because, well, how often does the average person ever get a chance to meet one?

So he was fawned over and made to feel special. But nearly everyone really despised him. He hadn't been much of a President, after all. He barely squeaked into office after his predecessor finished a very successful second term and couldn't run again. Bennett, on the other hand, tanked the economy and got the United States into a war with a former soviet bloc country for the worst of reasons. He didn't like the dictator who ran it.

So Bennett did what Presidents sometimes do. He misused his power and had his people develop falsified evidence, false testimony, that this nation was developing weapons capable of destroying Israel and the United States. It was all bullshit. But it's ridiculously easy to deceive a public who doesn't have access to the truth.

It's easy for a crooked politician, whose party controls both houses of congress, to mold the truth into whatever he wants it to be.

So Bennett did that. He sent American troops into a country that had no plans to attack either Israel or the United States. And had they wanted to, they didn't have the means to. What they did have, though, was a strong army which was fiercely loyal to its leader. Loyal enough to die for him. And they did, in vast numbers.

The problem was, they took a lot of Americans along with them. Over 3,000 of them. America's finest. Our sons and daughters. Dead on frozen battlefields half a world away. For nothing. Because Bennett didn't like the man who ran that country.

It wasn't the first time, of course, an American President had started a war for his own ideological reasons. Or to meet his own personal agenda.

It wasn't until Bennett was defeated by a landslide after his first term that rumors started to circulate. And it wasn't until the new President stopped the war and withdrew the American troops from the decimated country that inspectors discovered the extent of the fraud perpetrated on the American people.

UN inspectors discovered no weapons of mass destruction. No nuclear capability. No chemical weapons. No biological weapons. Just millions of rifles, rocket launchers and land mines. Defensive weapons. The kinds of weapons that could be used to ward off a rich, powerful country like the United States for a certain period of time. But not to be a threat to anyone.

And later, Bennett's real motives became known. *American Times Magazine* did an extensive investigation that took two years to complete. They discovered that the whole slew of them- Bennett, his relatives, his friends, friends of friends, all had invested heavily in the defense industry in the months leading up his taking office. Each one of them made tens of millions. So did the friends and families of the Vice President, the Chief of Staff and the Secretary of Defense. But the investments were so well hidden, so well sheltered in blind trusts and overseas reinvestments, that a final accounting was never completed.

And there was nothing illegal about it. That's what outraged Americans most of all. The blood money this group took in exchange for 3,000 American lives broke no rules.

So even though individually they fawned over him, Americans as a group grew to hate this man.

Bennett didn't let that stop him, of course. He did what disgraced politicians always do. He went to ground, stayed on the family ranch for a couple of years, and laid low. He waited for the dust to settle, for the smoke to clear. For people to forget.

Then he very slowly, very carefully, began to reintroduce himself to the public. He became a client of the best public relations firm in the country. They were famous for making the despicable appear tolerable. And they knew their stuff.

They started out by scheduling his appearances at the speaking engagements of other, more popular players. Long-term congressmen who enjoyed approval ratings of over seventy percent in their districts. Senators who were considered up and comers in their political party. Philanthropists who were famous for funding children's hospitals, or shelters for the homeless.

And at some point during each of these events, the cameras would record his presence in the group. Because, after all, he was a former President. And with his permanent detail of four secret service agents, he tended to stick out in a crowd.

And when asked for a comment or interview from a local television station or print reporter, he'd be careful to take the high road.

"Oh, this isn't about me," he'd say. "I'm just here to celebrate the opening of this wonderful new hospital for children's cancer patients."

The goal, of course, was to ease him back into the public spotlight. To make him palatable again. To encourage Americans to forget his transgressions, and bury the past. To let bygones be bygones.

If, a little at a time, he could be seen less and less as a heartless seller of American lives, and more as a misunderstood good guy, then he'd be able to reintegrate into society. Begin sitting on boards of big corporations again. Start rolling in even more and more millions to add to his already vast fortune.

And so it was that he came to be sitting in the audience at Mike Allen's anniversary dinner to celebrate his fortieth year in the United States Senate. He didn't sit at the head table, of course, although they'd offered it to him. He had a table toward the back of the banquet hall, where he could enter without much fanfare and make an early exit if the crowd appeared to be openly hostile toward him.

And it was while sitting at this table, while Allen was in the middle of expressing his gratitude for the people who put on the event, that Ron Bennett's heart exploded. Without warning.

He was dead instantly, of course. As his head fell into his bowl of soup, a secret service agent was on him immediately. Shielding him from further gunshots. A second agent helped him to the floor, where he'd be a harder target. A call went out on a hidden microphone, and the two remaining agents at the exits went on alert, scanning the rafters for threats. Then the crowd.

The first agent had the former President on the floor now, assessing his condition. He quickly determined that the President was dead. He had no respiration or pulse. His face was covered with chicken bisque soup, his eyes wide open.

The agent knew he was dead even before his head slumped. Otherwise his reflexes would have closed his eyes as his head fell forward.

He also quickly realized that Bennett was not felled with a bullet. There was simply no visible wound. He keyed his collar mike and turned his head to the left.

"It looks like natural causes and he's signal 60. Get an ambulance here quickly. No lights, no siren."

The cleansing had begun.

CPSIA information can be obtained at www.ICGtesting.com
Printed in the USA
LVOW07s1540290115

424893LV00003B/472/P